AF447821

Returns and Exchanges:

A jukebox musical comedy about retail

James Pavlick

Copyright © 2014 James Pavlick

All rights reserved.

ISBN: 9798687434201

DEDICATION

To Krista

Contents

ACKNOWLEDGMENTS

Thank you to all the musicians and their music that inspired me. I hope I give your songs proper credence and respect.

<u>CAST OF CHARACTERS</u>

The Main Characters will remain;
Add or remove extras as necessary.

AUGUST WINTERS: She is the main character.
                                   She is a listless wanderer
                                   and a college dropout. She
                                   works at the customer service
                                   desk. The story is told
                                   mostly by her perspective.
                                   Attractive and also a flirt. She
                                   is rapidly approaching her 22nd
                                   birthday

LLEWELLYN BROOKS "LEW":   A country boy and a
                                   supervisor at REALLY GOOD
                                   BUY. Wear cowboy boots
                                   instead of dress shoes, as
                                   per to company policy. He is
                                   a constant irritant to ROCK
                                   due to dress code violations.
                                   He has a crush on AUGUST. He
                                   is rapidly approaching the
                                   30's

JACKIE JONES, "J.J.":   Virginal and mousy, a stark
                                   contrast to AUGUST in terms
                                   of demeanor and looks. She is
                                   a front end clerk who works
                                   the Point of Sale (POS) cash
                                   register. She is a dreamer.
                                   She is in her mid-20's, older
                                   than AUGUST WINTERS

ROCK ROWLAND: A manager at REALLY GOOD BUY. He lives and breathes corporate policies which interferes with his personal life. He is best friend's with CHAD STEVENS; He is in his late 20's but younger than Llewellyn

RICKY O'BRIAN: An associate who works in the home television department. He believes he is God's gift to womankind and carries secret affairs with multiple women. A diamond stud adorns his left ear with blonde hair atop his head. He is barely 21 years old

CHAD STEVENS: A front end supervisor at REALLY GOOD BUY. He is best friends with ROCK ROWLAND. He is laid back and easy going. He is in his mid-20's

MARK MANN: The General Manager of REALLY GOOD BUY. Legend has it, he never speaks unless he is firing someone. Wear a white polo shirt. Age is unknown but obvious he is older than most

GEORGE ATKINS: Cantankerous older man who has been in the business of retail for 30+ years. He is in his late 50's

SALVATORE "PONY" MARSCAPONE: Bartender and owner of the
                                MACINTOSH CLUB. He is
                                ostentatious and has larger-
                                than-life personality. He is
                                in his late 40's

VAQUERA "VIQI" MARSCAPONE: Waitress at the MACINTOSH
                                CLUB and wife to PONY. She is
                                a free-spirited, wild child.
                                Her hair is dark with a pixie
                                cut. She is in her early 30's
                                and attractive

CUSTOMERS: A random assortment of people
                                With small speaking roles;
                                all male; all are in their
                                late 30's and 40's

REALLY GOOD BUY EMPLOYEES: A random assortment of people
                                With small speaking roles,
                                mostly male (3-7). They are
                                all in their early 20's or
                                late teens

BAR PATRONS: A random assortment of bar
                                enthusiasts at the MACINTOSH
                                CLUB; Can double as RGB EMPLOYEES

THE SETTING

<u>TIME</u>

In the near future

<u>PLACE</u>

Broomfield, a suburb of Denver, CO

<u>SCENES</u>

VISTA WINDOWS APARTMENTS:	Dormitory-style apartments dedicated for all employees of REALLY GOOD BUY. All employees except managers and supervisors live here. It is located across the street from REALLY GOOD BUY. Their logo is an open window
REALLY GOOD BUY:	A big-box retail location that sells electronics, appliances, musical instruments, car audio decks, and computers. The uniforms are green polo shirts with khaki slacks. They are in competition with another big box retailer with a yellow tag logo. REALLY is colored in red. GOOD is colored in green. BUY is colored in blue

MACINTOSH CLUB: A popular bar/club with a large dance floor and a long bar attended by a fiery Italian proprietor and his Spanish wife. Its logo is an apple with a bite taken out of both sides, asymmetrically It is located in the same parking lot as REALLY GOOD BUY

THE BACKGROUND

REALLY GOOD BUY, the WINDOWS VISTA APARTMENTS, and the MACINTOSH CLUB are all owned and operated by the same corporation. This is implicit; no mention that the same corporation owns all components of the setting beset for the musical.

Every employee lives at the Windows Vista Apartments. Every employee works for Really Good Buy. Most employees relax at the Macintosh Club. All three buildings are within a two-minute walking distance from each other.

THE SET LIST

ACT 1

1. Salt Sweat Sugar – Jimmy Eat World............................ *August*
2. The Man Comes Around – Johnny Cash............................ *Llewellyn*
3. I Will Wait – Mumford & Sons................................. *Llewellyn*
4. I'm So Sick – Flyleaf....................................... *Jackie*
5. Sex Type Thing – Stone Temple Pilots........................ *Ricky*
6. We're Not Going to Take It – Twisted Sister… *August, Chad*
7. Where Is My Mind? – Yoav.................................... *Jackie, Chad*
8. My Curse – Killswitch Engage............................... *August*
9. All My Life – Foo Fighters................................. *Ricky*
10.   Scream With Me – Mudvayne.............................. *August*
11.   Tainted Love – Marilyn Manson......................... *August*

ACT 2

1. Call Me When You're Sober – Evanescence............ *August*
2. All the Love in the World – Nine Inch Nails… *Jackie*
3. Get Lucky – Daft Punk...................................... *Ricky, August, Pony, Viqi*
4. The End – Kings of Leon.................................... *Rock*
5. Breaking the Girl – Red Hot Chili Peppers......... *Pony*
6. Oil and Water – Incubus.................................... *Jackie*
7. Beware – Deftones.. *Llewellyn*
8. Licking Cream – Sevendust.................................. *Ricky, August*
9. Lose Yourself to Dance – Daft Punk......................... *Jackie, Rock*
10.   Hurt – Johnny Cash.................................... *Llewellyn*
11.   The Pot – Tool.. *Mark Mann*
12.   The Man Comes Around – Johnny Cash.............. *Ricky*
13.   Fix You – Coldplay.................................... *Everyone*

ACT 1:

Salt, Sweat, Sugar

[***SET TRANSITION****: Lighting shows a disheveled bedroom. Beer bottles and alcohol bottles are littering the floor along with discarded clothing. A television is turned on and playing music videos in the background. The bed is tucked into the corner of the bedroom near STAGE LEFT. A large clock with red numbers ticks silently STAGE RIGHT. It is meant to display the 'real' time in the play. The time displayed is 8:59]*

(A woman is sleeping on the bed. There is a knock on the door. It is a woman knocking. She is wearing a green polo uniform shirt and khaki pants)

AUGUST:

(shouts)
What?

JACKIE JONES:

Hello, it's J.J. May I come in?

AUGUST:

(sighs heavily)
I've got my tits out.

J.J.

Well then, um…please put something on! Then may I come in?
(she hesitates before she opens the door and sits down on the edge of the bed. She folds her hands across her lap)

AUGUST:

(She lifts her bed sheet to cover herself while she searches for a t-shirt. She finds one and puts it on)
What is it? What do you want?

    J.J.

    (recoils)
Oh, nothing really. I just wanted to come and chat.
    (looks at AUGUST)
You look like H-E double hockey sticks.

    AUGUST:

Yeah, I got in late last night from the uh, the Mac Club.

    J.J.:

Are you not feeling well?

    AUGUST:

Among other things, yeah. I haven' been this hungover in a
while…

    J.J.:

    (smiles timidly)
I-I could've sworn I heard you bringing home a boy, too. Who was
it?

    AUGUST:

    (smiles sheepishly, looks away)
I-I don't know what you're talking about.

    J.J.:

    (scoffs)
Oh, come *on*. I heard him talking last night. He was practically
shouting when he was in here with you.

    AUGUST:

Okay, okay, yeah. I had a guy over.
    (throws her hands in the air for a shrug)

J.J.:

You seem to always have boys over.

AUGUST:

Yeah, well, if you weren't a little goody two-shoes all the
frickin' time, you can have guys over too. I think it's because
I trace my fingers down their spine, like I'm crawling down it.
It drives them wild!
     (points to J.J.'s chest)
You do have a nice body by the way.

J.J.:

     (blushes)
Thank you.

AUGUST:

Since you're into all that ballet, you should bust out one of
those outfits some time. It's hot. Or maybe if you brought out
that little red bag you've stashed away in your closet every
once in a while…

J.J.:

     (shouting)
I've asked, no told, you nicely: stay out of my room! That is
none of your business! I don't even know why I bought it.

AUGUST:

     (laughing)
It's because you've got a little freak in you. You should let it
out sometime. I'm sure it's suffocating under your clothes.

J.J.:

(standing, shouting)
Just please stay out of my room!
(leaves, slams the door)

AUGUST:

Jesus, she's wound tight. Piano wire could take a lesson.

J.J.:

(opens the bedroom door and pokes her head in)
I heard that! By the way, it's 9:04.
(smiles devilishly and closes the door, EXIT STAGE RIGHT)

AUGUST:

9:04? 9:04! Damn……I'm late!

(in a whirlwind, AUGUST leaps from the bed and frantically changes from her t-shirt to her work uniform) {Nudity optional}

[The TV changes to Salt, Sweat, Sugar by Jimmy Eat World. The video pauses when AUGUST pauses]

I'M NOT ALONE CAUSE THE TV'S ON, YEAH.
(turns off the TV)
I'M NOT CRAZY 'CAUSE I TAKE THE RIGHT PILLS EVERY DAY.
(finds a bottle of pills, opens it, and takes a handful)
AND REST, CLEAN YOUR CONSCIENCE,
(shakes her head)
CLEAR YOUR THOUGHTS WITH SPEYSIDE WITH YOUR GRAIN.
(takes a pull from a bottle of beer)
CLEAN YOUR CONSCIENCE; CLEAR YOUR THOUGHTS WITH SPEYSIDE.
(tosses clothes aside to find her pants, a pair of tan khakis)
SALT, SWEAT, SUGAR ON THE ASPHALT.
OUR HEARTS LITTERING THE TOPSOIL.
(she picks up a shirt. It is obvious it is not hers but a man's instead)

TUNE IN AND WE CAN GET THE LAST CALL.
OUR LIVES, OUR COAL.
    (More rummaging leads her to find her green polo. It
    is the same polo as the one J.J. wore)
SALT, SWEAT, SUGAR ON THE ASPHALT.
OUR HEARTS LITTERING THE TOPSOIL.
    (she puts on the polo)
SIGN UP IT'S THE PICKET LINE OR THE PARADE.
OUR LIVES.
    (She checks herself in a tall floor mirror briefly before
    exiting the bedroom, STAGE RIGHT. The lighting turns off,
    sending the stage into darkness)

    [END SCENE]

The Man Comes Around

[**SET TRANSITION:** *The audience is shown the inside of REALLY GOOD BUY. Near STAGE RIGHT is a checkout lane. A small soda machine sits in front of the checkout lane, perpendicular to the desk. Near STAGE LEFT is the customer service desk. In the middle is the entrance/exit of REALLY GOOD BUY. Several employees including J.J., CHAD, and LLEWELLYN are standing near the entrance to RGB. AUGUST enters through the entrance, disheveled and winded]*

LLEWELLYN:

(laughing)
Well look who decided to show up for her shift!

AUGUST:

(out of breath)
Sorry I'm late. Has Mann been by yet?

CHAD:

(scoffs)
You're lucky. No, he hasn't been by yet.

(A man appears from STAGE RIGHT. He is dressed in a white shirt and tan khakis. In his hand, a clipboard with yellow sheets. He walks slowly without a word)

LLEWELLYN:

Speak of the devil…

CHAD:

…and he shall appear.

J.J.:

You know, I do believe I have never heard him speak before. It's always been Rock that delivers the morning break-outs, not Mr. Mann.

CHAD:

Legend has it, Mann never speaks. His voice is so powerful; it would deafen us ALL if he did!
(shouts ALL before lowering his voice)

LLEWELLYN:

Keep your voice down, idiot! He'll, like, hear you and do something…dastardly.

CHAD:

As I understand it, he only talks to Rock for some reason.
(scoffs, exits STAGE RIGHT)

AUGUST:

Come to think of it, I've never heard him speak either.

J.J.:

I've heard another legend. There is that one legend that he doesn't hand out pink slips but ones printed on golden sheets instead. Isn't that kind of strange?

ROCK, OFF STAGE:

Come and see the breakout, team!

          LLEWELLYN:

And I heard, as it were, the noise of thunder. One of the four
beasts saying, 'Come and see.' and I saw, and behold a white
horse.
          (he gestures to MANN)

THERE'S A MAN GOIN' 'ROUND TAKIN' NAMES,
AND HE DECIDES WHO TO FREE AND WHO TO BLAME.
EVERYBODY WON'T BE TREATED ALL THE SAME,
THERE'LL BE A GOLDEN LADDER REACHIN' DOWN.
WHEN THE MAN COMES AROUND.
          *(the man walks past the employees, barely
          acknowledging them as he passes by)*
          (__pause__)
THE HAIRS ON YOUR ARM WILL STAND UP,
          *(LLEWELLYN grabs J.J.'s arm and runs his fingers up
          her arm)*
AT THE TERROR IN EACH SIP AND IN EACH SUP.
WILL YOU PARTAKE OF THAT LAST OFFERED CUP,
          (he points to the ground)
OR DISAPPEAR INTO THE POTTER'S GROUND?
WHEN THE MAN COMES AROUND.
          *(MANN returns from STAGE RIGHT, walking slowly passed
          the employees. He is scribbling furiously on his
          clipboard)*
HEAR THE TRUMPETS HEAR THE PIPERS.
ONE HUNDRED MILLION ANGELS SINGIN'.
MULTITUDES ARE MARCHIN' TO THE BIG KETTLEDRUM.
VOICES CALLIN', VOICES CRYIN'.
SOME ARE BORN AND SOME ARE DYIN'.
IT'S ALPHA AND OMEGA'S KINGDOM COME,

          (MANN pauses to look at J.J. and AUGUST)

          ←*crucial that MANN looks at J.J. then AUGUST)*

AND THE WHIRLWIND IS IN THE THORN TREE.
          *(MANN points to their shirt tails. They are untucked.
          AUGUST and J.J. frantically tuck in their shirts to
          match the other employees)*
THE VIRGINS ARE ALL TRIMMING THEIR WICKS,

THE WHIRLWIND IS IN THE THORN TREE.
IT'S HARD FOR THEE TO KICK AGAINST THE PRICKS,
> *(LLEWELLYN motions towards an unnamed employee, a young man with a diamond stud in his ear. He winks at AUGUST as he walks away towards STAGE RIGHT. AUGUST rolls her eyes as he passes; he exits STAGE RIGHT)*

AUGUST:

> *(scoffs)*

Ugh, I can't stand Ricky.

J.J.:

I don't know, I think he's sort of cute, in a devil may care sort of way.

AUGUST:

> *(turns to J.J.)*

Oh yeah? If you're so in love with him, why don't you ever go and talk to him?

J.J.:

I do, all the time. I mean, I say hello to him when I can but I mean something else. You know how it is.

AUGUST:

> *(laughing)*

Yeah, all too well. Always in retail: we say one thing when we mean something else.
LLEWELLYN:

I definitely know what you mean.
> *(smirks and smiles at AUGUST)*

> *(AUGUST ignore LLEWELLYN)*

ROCK, OFF STAGE:

What's this, a moss patch? Break it up people, the store's about
to open. August, can you come here? I need your help.

AUGUST:

Coming!

*(AUGUST walks towards and behind the customer service desk
to talk with ROCK. Their dialogue is inaudible)*

J.J.:

(muttering)
I'm sure you were. Why does she get all the love in the world?

LLEWELLYN:

(turns to J.J. after watching AUGUST walking away)
What was that?

J.J.:

What? Oh, nothing! Time for work!

*(J.J. averts her eyes and walks behind the checkout lane.
LLEWELLYN changes his gaze from J.J. back to AUGUST and
ROCK; he watches them talk)*

*[MANN walks around the store randomly throughout Act   He
never speak to the employees, only points]*

I Will Wait

LLEWELLYN:

Is she dating anyone?
        (points to AUGUST)

J.J.:

(not paying attention)
Who, Rock? I'm fairly certain he's straight, Lew.

LLEWELLYN:

No, not Rock, dingus. I'm straight too. Gah, never mind.
        (throws his hands in the air and starts to exit STAGE
        RIGHT)

J.J.:

(laughing)
I know what you meant. I was kidding. No, she's not dating
anyone. That I know of, I mean.

LLEWELLYN:

That you know of?
        (raises eyebrows)

J.J.:

What? I didn't say that. No, she doesn't have a boyfriend.
        (looks away)
Why don't you go talk to her?

LLEWELLYN:

I-I don't even know what to say to her.

J.J.:

Just say what you think. Of her, I mean.
(starts playing with the cash register)

LLEWELLYN:

Well, I'm her boss, technically. Supervisor anyways. I know there's no rule about supervisors dating subordinates like there is about managers dating them. I just clam up, I guess.

J.J.:

Stop being a sissy and go talk to her. Tell her what's on your mind. Just remember, what's on your mind and what you say are two different things. She'll be able to tell the difference.
(ROCK exits STAGE LEFT)
See? Rock's gone. You won't get in trouble now. Go. Go!
(shoos away LLEWELLYN)

(LLEWELLYN walks slowly towards the customer service desk. He straightens his shirt and presses down on his pants, wiping the sweat from his hands. AUGUST is going about her morning, organizing and preparing for the opening of the store)

[The red clock reads 9:55]

LLEWELLYN:

H-hey August.

AUGUST:

Hey Lew.

LLEWELLYN:

(exhales slowly)
O-kay. Here goes nothing. I have this idea of how we would work
when...or *OR* if you and I started dating.
(stammering towards the end)

AUGUST:

Oh yeah? How would that go?
*(AUGUST leaves the customer service desk and stands in
front of LLEWELLYN)*

[**SET TRANSITION:** *The lighting begins to change, giving the
stage a dream-like feel. Cooler colors. LLEWELLYN begins to
sing]*

LLEWELLYN:

WELL, I CAME HOME
LIKE A STONE
AND I FELL HEAVY INTO YOUR ARMS
(LLEWELLYN falls into AUGUST's open arms)
THESE DAYS OF DUST
WHICH WE'VE KNOWN
*(LLEWELLYN stands back up and sweeps his right arm
across, gesturing towards the store)*
WILL BLOW AWAY WITH THIS NEW SUN
(pause)
BUT I'LL KNEEL DOWN,
*(LLEWELLYN kneels down before AUGUST in a mock
proposal)*
WAIT FOR NOW
AND I'LL KNEEL DOWN,
KNOW MY GROUND
*(AUGUST draws her hands to her face. She is in shock
from his proposal but says nothing)*
AND I WILL WAIT, I WILL WAIT FOR YOU
AND I WILL WAIT, I WILL WAIT FOR YOU
*(**pause**)*

SO BREAK MY STEP
AND RELENT
WELL, YOU FORGAVE AND I WON'T FORGET
KNOW WHAT WE'VE SEEN
AND HIM WITH LESS
NOW IN SOME WAY SHAKE THE EXCESS
      (LLEWELLYN stands with no answer from AUGUST)
'CAUSE I WILL WAIT, I WILL WAIT FOR YOU
AND I WILL WAIT, I WILL WAIT FOR YOU
      (LLEWELLYN takes AUGUST's hand and twirls her into his
     arms)
AND I WILL WAIT, I WILL WAIT FOR YOU
AND I WILL WAIT, I WILL WAIT FOR YOU
     (pause*)*
NOW I'LL BE BOLD
AS WELL AS STRONG
     (flexes his arms)
AND USE MY HEAD ALONGSIDE MY HEART
     (touches his head then covers his heart with an
     imaginary cowboy hat)
SO TAME MY FLESH
AND FIX MY EYES
A TETHERED MIND FREED FROM THE LIES
     (sweeps his right arm across the store)
AND I'LL KNEEL DOWN,
WAIT FOR NOW
I'LL KNEEL DOWN,
     (kneels down again)
KNOW MY GROUND
     (pause*)*
RAISE MY HANDS
     (proposes again)
PAINT MY SPIRIT GOLD
AND BOW MY HEAD
(bows his head)
KEEP MY HEART SLOW
     (AUGUST begins to nod emphatically, wiping away
     'tears' as LLEWELLYN places an imaginary ring on her
     hand. LLEWELLYN stands and pumps his fist in the air)
Yeehaw!

*(He twirls her close and into his arms again, this
time dancing slower. They kiss and he un-twirls her.
AUGUST begins to walk back behind the customer service
desk)*
'CAUSE I WILL WAIT, I WILL WAIT FOR YOU
AND I WILL WAIT, I WILL WAIT FOR YOU
(singing grows more faint as she walks away)
AND I WILL WAIT, I WILL WAIT FOR YOU
And I will wait, I will wait for you…

*(AUGUST returns to the desk and continues her tasks as
before. The entire scene was in LLEWELLYN's head)*

AUGUST:

(looks up from her task)
Hmm? Did you need something?

LLEWELLYN:

N-no. I mean, yes. No. Just wanted to come over and say hey.
Store's opening. I'll talk to you later.

[The clock reads 10:00]

[END SCENE]

I'm So Sick

[BEGIN SCENE]

    [The clock reads 10:01]

    (A few customers stroll in through the entrance/exit of the
    store. J.J. greets them as they walk in. She watches as
    LLEWELLYN walks away towards the customer service desk. She
    smirks as he stands there awkwardly as she goes about her
    tasks for the morning)

    J.J.:

I WILL BREAK INTO YOUR THOUGHTS
WITH WHAT'S WRITTEN ON MY HEART
I WILL BREAK, BREAK

    (The first customer of the day walks in through the
    entrance, turns towards the checkout lane and to the
    soda machine. He selects a soda and walks towards
    J.J.)

    Customer #1:

Hello there.
    (hands J.J. the soda)
    (J.J. attempts to scan the soda several times to no avail)

    Customer #1:

    (laughing)
Uh oh. It doesn't scan. That must mean it's free!

    J.J.:

    (smiles weakly)
I'M SO SICK,
INFECTED WITH WHERE I LIVE
LET ME LIVE WITHOUT THIS
EMPTY BLISS,
SELFISHNESS

(laughs weakly)
Um yeah, no. Not free.
    (the item finally scans. J.J. rings out the customer)
Have a good day!
    (the customer leaves. J.J. continues)
I'M SO SICK
I'M SO SICK

    *(another customer approaches with a small product in
    his hand. J.J. rings him out)*

IF YOU WANT MORE OF THIS
WE CAN PUSH OUT, SELL OUT, DIE OUT
SO YOU'LL SHUT UP
AND STAY SLEEPING
WITH MY SCREAMING IN YOUR ITCHING EARS

    *(a third customer approaches with two products in his hand.
    He smiles at J.J. and leans on the desk as she rings him
    out)*

    J.J.:

Here's your receipt, sir.
    (smiles weakly)

    Customer #3:

    (smugly)
Thanks beautiful. I'm missing one thing though
    (points to the bottom of the receipt)

    J.J.:

Oh, did I miss something?
    (looks down)

    Customer #3:

Yeah, your phone number. You didn't write your phone number
down.

J.J.:

(smile disappears)
Oh, I'm sorry sir but I…I don't date customers.

*(customer #3 frowns and leaves with his products in a small
green bag)*

J.J.:

I'M SO SICK,
INFECTED WITH WHERE I LIVE
LET ME LIVE WITHOUT THIS
EMPTY BLISS,
SELFISHNESS
I'M SO SICK
I'M SO SICK

(CHAD enters from STAGE LEFT)

HEAR IT, I'M SCREAMING IT
YOU'RE HEEDING TO IT NOW

HEAR IT! I'M SCREAMING IT!
YOU TREMBLE AT THIS SOUND

(J.J. helps another customer)

YOU SINK INTO MY CLOTHES
AND THIS INVASION
MAKES ME FEEL
WORTHLESS, HOPELESS, SICK

CHAD:

Hey hey J.J.!

J.J.:

Hello Chad.

CHAD:

How's the day treating you?

J.J.:

I'm so sick,
Infected with where I live
Let me live without this
Empty bliss,
Selfishness
I'm so sick
I'm so sick

CHAD:

J.J.? Earth to J.J., come in J.J.!

J.J.:

I'M SO SICK
INFECTED WITH WHERE I LIVE
LET ME LIVE WITHOUT THIS
EMPTY BLISS, SELFISHNESS
I'M SO
I'M SO SICK
I'M SO
I'M SO SICK

(J.J. ends her inner monologue to speak)

…It's going okay, I guess. How about yourself?

CHAD:

(shrugs)
Just another beautiful day in the life of retail. Keep those
sales up! We've got a big budget today. I'll check up on you
later.
(waves goodbye, exits STAGE RIGHT)

(CUSTOMER #4 enters from the entrance with a product in his hand. He means to return it)

[END SCENE]

Sex Type Thing

[***SET TRANSITION:*** *Home theater department. Several flat screen televisions adorn television stands. A checkout lane is near STAGE RIGHT. It stands perpendicular to the 'wall' of televisions. Several RGB employees are crowded around a single character. A customer meanders in the background as the employees talk to one another and to the single character, RICKY. The red clock reads 12:06]*

(Several employees clamor as RICKY raises his hands to silence them)

EMPLOYEE #1:

Saw you at the club with her last night.
   (winks)

EMPLOYEE #2:

Did you go back to your room with her last night?
   (elbows RICKY playfully)

   RICKY:

   (laughing)
Gentleman, I don't kiss and tell. But yeah, I took her back to her room, actually.

   EMPLOYEE #3:

   (whistles)
She's a pistol in the sack, I hear. Isn't she the village bicycle though?

   RICKY:

   (laughing continues)
You're new here, right?

EMPLOYEE #3:

(points to himself)
Me? Yeah, started two days ago. I've been training with this one
(points to EMPLOYEE #1)

RICKY:

Jesus, word travels fast. Yeah, she's the bicycle.

EMPLOYEE #1:

Yeah, I'll second that.
(guiltily looks away)

EMPLOYEE #3:

Well, if it's anything like my old retail job, this place is like a gigantic high school. Word definitely travels fast.

EMPLOYEE #2:

Legend has it, Ricky, so are you but for the ladies.

RICKY:

(scoffs)
Nah, man. I'm no bicycle. I'm more like, uh, like a pogo stick.
(everyone laughs)
Besides, I just choose my ladies carefully. Any lady is fair game…'cept J.J. That girl's so wound tight, she's practically a stone's throw away from starting a nun factory or something. Piano wire could take a lesson.

EMPLOYEE #1:

Isn't that what she said at the club last night?

RICKY:

(laughing)
Yeah, she totally did.

EMPLOYEE #3:

So what did you tell her to turn her into a beast with two
backs?

RICKY:

What, are you taking notes on how to pick her up?

EMPLOYEE #3:

(pauses)
Uh, well yeah, kinda. She's hot!

RICKY:

Well okay then. Listen up!
*(RICKY begins to walk around the home theater
department. He is dancing and makes suggestive dance
moves and hand gestures as he sings)*
I AM, I AM, I AM
I SAID I WANNA GET NEXT TO YOU
I SAID I GONNA GET CLOSE TO YOU
YOU WOULDN'T WANT ME HAVE TO HURT YOU TOO, HURT YOU TOO?

(RICKY pauses his singing to speak)

At this point, she's pretending she's totally not into me even
though she totally is. I could tell. I buy her drinks. Then
she's crossin' and uncrossin' those long stems underneath that
dress of hers. This is how I say it:

I AIN'T, I AIN'T, I AIN'T
A BUYIN' INTO YOUR APATHY
I'M GONNA LEARN YA MY PHILOSOPHY
YOU WANNA KNOW ABOUT ATROCITY, ATROCITY?

I KNOW YOU WANT WHAT'S ON MY MIND
I KNOW YOU LIKE WHAT'S ON MY MIND
I KNOW IT EATS YOU UP INSIDE
I KNOW, YOU KNOW, YOU KNOW, YOU KNOW

(A customer approached the four employees. He watches RICKY as he dances inappropriately and sings to the other three before he interrupts)

CUSTOMER #5:

Um, can I get some help over here?

RICKY:

Uh yeah, someone will be right with you. I'm almost done.
     (turns to the other employees)
Can you believe the nerve of that guy? Interrupting me? Where was I?
Oh yeah:
I AM A MAN, A MAN
I'LL GIVE YA SOMETHIN' THAT YA WON'T FORGET
I SAID YA SHOULDN'T HAVE WORN THAT DRESS
I SAID YA SHOULDN'T HAVE WORN THAT DRESS

By this point, we're both good and sauced. My apartment's on the third floor. Her apartment's on the first floor. Write that down.
     (points to EMPLOYEE #3. EMPLOYEE #3 furiously scribbles on a piece of scrap paper)
Naturally we want to save our…energy so we opt for her place. Then I says to her:

I KNOW YOU WANT WHAT'S ON MY MIND
I KNOW YOU LIKE WHAT'S ON MY MIND
I KNOW IT EATS YOU UP INSIDE
I KNOW, YOU KNOW, YOU KNOW, YOU KNOW

Now we're gettin' down and dirty:

HERE I COME, I COME, I COME

I AM, I AM, I AM
I SAID I WANNA GET NEXT TO YOU
I SAID I GONNA GET CLOSE TO YOU

Turns out she's a bit of a freak too:

YOU WOULDN'T WANT ME HAVE TO HURT YOU TOO, HURT YOU TOO?

She wants a little pillow talk. So here's what I got for her:

I KNOW YOU WANT WHAT'S ON MY MIND
I KNOW YOU LIKE WHAT'S ON MY MIND
I KNOW IT EATS YOU UP INSIDE
I KNOW, YOU KNOW, YOU KNOW, YOU KNOW
I KNOW YOU WANT WHAT'S ON MY MIND
I KNOW YOU LIKE WHAT'S ON MY MIND
I KNOW IT EATS YOU UP INSIDE
I KNOW, YOU KNOW, YOU KNOW, YOU KNOW

We throw back some beers on her bed, rehydrate and reenergize
before we go back at it. Then it's her then me then her then me
all…night…long
HERE I COME, I COME, I COME
HERE I COME, I COME, I COME
HERE I COME, I COME, I COME
HERE I COME, I COME, I COME

    EMPLOYEE #3:

Wow. That sounds awesome!

    RICKY:

New guy, you have no idea. Pistol indeed. She left me unloaded.
    (RICKY turns his fingers into a gun and shoots at EMPLOYEE
    #3 before turning towards the patiently waiting customer)
How can I help you?

    (EMPLOYEES 1-3 high five each other as RICKY walks away to
    assist the CUSTOMER. The CUSTOMER and RICKY's dialogue is
    inaudible. The MANN appears and EMPLOYEES 1-3 quickly
    disperse)

[END SCENE]

We're Not Going to Take It

[**SET TRANSITION**: *REALLY GOOD BUY customer service desk. It is a large black, L-shaped desk separating the clerk from the customer. The L is inverted so that the long part of the desk is perpendicular to the audience. The DESK and CLERK face STAGE RIGHT. There is a single Point of Sale (POS) register on this DESK. Behind the DESK, illegible by the audience, is the REALLY GOOD BUY terms and conditions on returns and exchanges]*

(AUGUST is standing behind the REALLY GOOD BUY customer service desk. She is bored and playing on her phone. SHE is wearing a headset that is connected to a walkie talkie. CUSTOMER #4 walks up with a boxed product in his hand. He intends to return it]

AUGUST:

(To CUSTOMER #4)
Hello sir, welcome to Really Good Buy. How can I help you?

CUSTOMER #4:

(To AUGUST)
Yeah, uh, I'd like to make a return.
        (HE places the product onto the desk)

AUGUST:

Okay then, I can help you with that. May I ask what's wrong with it?

CUSTOMER #4:

Yeah, it don' turn on.

AUGUST:

Um, okay. Did you plug it first?

CUSTOMER #4:

(Pause)
Do you think I'm an idiot?

AUGUST:

No, of course not!
 (AUGUST looks towards the audience with a look on her face)

CUSTOMER #4:

(Shouting)
No, I didn't plug it in!

AUGUST:

Okay, well, do you want to plug it in? It probably works if you just tried…

CUSTOMER #4:

(Shouting continues)
No, you idiot! I want to return it!

AUGUST:

(Unfazed)
Okee dokee then. Do you have a receipt?

CUSTOMER #4:

No, I don' have a receipt!

AUGUST:

Oh, that's going to be a problem.
 (Points to the wall behind her)

CUSTOMER #4:

What's that say?

AUGUST:

(AUGUST looks back at the audience with a look on her face)
It basically says no receipt, no return.

CUSTOMER #4:

Wait, what? What does that mean?

AUGUST:

Well, it means…
OH WE'RE NOT GONNA TAKE IT
NO, WE AIN'T GONNA TAKE IT
OH WE'RE NOT GONNA TAKE IT ANYMORE

CUSTOMER #4:

(shouting)
You can't do that!

AUGUST:

WE'VE GOT THE RIGHT TO CHOOSE AND
THERE AIN'T NO WAY WE'LL LOSE IT
THIS IS OUR LIFE, THIS IS OUR SONG
WE'LL FIGHT THE POWERS THAT BE JUST
DON'T PICK OUR DESTINY 'CAUSE
YOU DON'T KNOW US, YOU DON'T BELONG

CUSTOMER #4:

(Still shouting)
Okay, that's it! I demand to speak to a manager!

AUGUST:

(Smiling, SHE speaks into her walkie talkie headset)
Hey Chad, could you swing by customer service? I've got a
customer that would like to give you a shout.

*[CHAD STEVENS enters the stage from STAGE LEFT and walks
towards the DESK. HE stands next to AUGUST and faces
CUSTOMER #4]*

CHAD:

Hello sir, welcome to Really Good Buy. How can I help you?

CUSTOMER #4:

(shouting, point to AUGUST)
This bitch won' return my product!

CHAD:

Well, that just plain unfortunate. Before we get started, please
refrain from profanity or else I'll be forced to ask you to
leave.

CUSTOMER #4:

Okay fine. I want to return this.
(Slams box down against desk)

CHAD:

I would love to, sir. Do you have a receipt?

CUSTOMER #4:

No, I *don't* have a receipt

CHAD:

Oh, that's unfortunate. Did she point to the wall?

CUSTOMER #4:

Yeah, she pointed to the wall.

CHAD:

Did she sing the song?

CUSTOMER #4:

Well, yeah. She sang the song. What's that got to do with it?

CHAD:

Oh well, it's simple really:

CHAD, AUGUST (together):

OH WE'RE NOT GONNA TAKE IT
NO, WE AIN'T GONNA TAKE IT
OH WE'RE NOT GONNA TAKE IT ANYMORE

CUSTOMER #4:

(screaming)
This is bullshit! Do you know how much money I spend here?! That
entitles me to special treatment! I deserve special treatment!

CHAD:

OH YOU'RE SO CONDESCENDING
YOUR GALL IS NEVER ENDING
WE DON'T WANT NOTHIN', NOT A THING FROM YOU
YOUR LIFE IS TRITE AND JADED
BORING AND CONFISCATED
IF THAT'S YOUR BEST, YOUR BEST WON'T DO

(CHAD stops singing to talk to CUSTOMER #4)
If you do so much business with us, then you would know what the
return policy is. I warned you about the use of profanity. Now
please leave my store before I have you escorted out.
(Points towards the 'door')

CUSTOMER #4:

(Grabs his box)
[CUSTOMER #4 exits STAGE RIGHT]

CHAD:

(CHAD waits until CUSTOMER #4 leaves)
You weren't kidding about the shouting.

AUGUST:

Yeah, no kidding. Thanks for your help. Where you off to now?

CHAD:

I'm going to swing by the front lanes, give J.J. a howdy-do, see
what's on her mind.

AUGUST:

(Laughing)
Something tells me you want to give her more than a howdy-do. I
know what's on your mind.

CHAD:

(Scowling)
Yeah yeah shut up and get back to work.

*(CHAD walks away from AUGUST towards the checkout lane
and J.J.)*

where is my mind?

(CHAD saunters slowly towards J.J. J.J. is busy day dreaming with her chin on her hand)

[The red clock reads 1:15]

CHAD:

Busted!

J.J.:

(looks up in a daze)
Hmm? What? Oh, I uh-

CHAD:

Don't even sweat it. We're slow now anyways.

J.J.:

I'm sorry, what? What are we talking about?

CHAD:

(laughing)
Oh *wow*. You were day dreaming *hard*!

J.J.:

Yeah. It can get a little boring up here sometimes.

CHAD:

Boring? In retail? Nah, that's unheard of! This place is a three-ring circus!

J.J.:

(smiles weakly)
Sorry about that. I won't let my mind wander so far again.

*(another customer walks up and places a product on the
checkout lane counter. CHAD steps aside. She rings out the
customer and s/he goes on their way)*

CHAD:

(repeats)
I won't let my mind wander so far again. Where did your mind go?
Where was your mind then? Where is your mind now?
(leans against the checkout lane counter)

J.J.:

(looks away sheepishly, whispers)
Um, doing cartwheels.

CHAD:

That's adorable.
(smiles)

J.J.:

What about you? Where is your mind?

CHAD:

(pauses, then smiles)
Somewhere tropical, I think. With warm, sandy beaches and the
ocean.

J.J.:

(sighs slowly)
That sounds amazing…

         CHAD:

Hell, that's where I am right now.

         [**SET TRANSITION:** *the set of RGB breaks away to reveal
         a tropical backdrop. The lighting will change to
         reflect a warmer, tropical feel. All characters leave
         the set except CHAD and J.J. They are still dressed in
         their RGB green polo and khaki pant uniforms for the
         time being]*

         *(CHAD and J.J. start several feet away from each
         other. They remain static but only for a short time.
         They will begin a slow waltz but only after J.J. moves
         into CHAD as he sings)*

WITH YOUR FEET ON THE AIR AND YOUR HEAD ON THE GROUND
         (points up then down, respectively)
         (J.J. does a cartwheel then falls into CHAD's arms)
TRY THIS TRICK AND SPIN IT, YEAH
         *(CHAD slowly twirls J.J. out, straightening their arms
         before CHAD pulls J.J. back into his arms)*
YOUR HEAD WILL COLLAPSE
         (points to J.J.'s head)
BUT THERE'S NOTHING IN IT
AND YOU'LL ASK YOURSELF
   (slow waltz continues)

WHERE IS MY MIND?
   (CHAD touches his own head)

WHERE IS MY MIND?
         (CHAD slides his hand down from his head)
WHERE IS MY MIND?

         *(J.J. steps away from CHAD, pushing him away, and slowly
         walks in sweeping strides of her legs, almost ballet-like.
         She begins to slowly strip away her uniform to reveal a
         non-revealing one piece swimsuit. She begins to dance on
         her own, ballet)*

J.J.:

I WAS SWIMMIN' IN THE CARIBBEAN
ANIMALS WERE HIDING BEHIND THE ROCKS
EXCEPT THE LITTLE FISH
BUT THEY TOLD ME, HE SWEARS
TRYIN' TO TALK TO ME, TO ME, TO ME.

J.J., CHAD:

(standing away from each other, facing away)
WHERE IS MY MIND?
WHERE IS MY MIND?
WHERE IS MY MIND?

WAY OUT IN THE WATER
SEE IT SWIMMIN'

WHERE IS MY MIND?

Way out in the water
See it swimmin'

WHERE IS MY MIND?
WHERE IS MY MIND?
WHERE IS MY MIND?

CHAD:

WHERE IS MY MIND?

[**SET TRANSITION:** *The lighting changes from the cool blues to warmer colors: yellows, oranges, and reds. The transition will affect the physical set. This is to represent the change in 'mindset' of CHAD]*

(J.J. begins to change from her traditional ballet to a more aggressive 'rock' ballet to reflect the change in tempo in the music. Because CHAD does not know ballet and is only a classically trained ballroom dancer, he can only stand back, watch, and enjoy)

WITH YOUR FEET ON THE AIR AND YOUR HEAD ON THE GROUND
TRY THIS TRICK AND SPIN IT, YEAH
YOUR HEAD WILL COLLAPSE
IF THERE'S NOTHING IN IT
AND YOU'LL ASK YOURSELF

WHERE IS MY MIND?
WHERE IS MY MIND?
WHERE IS MY MIND?

     (CHAD walks closer to J.J. She walks away slow, towards the
     audience as she sings)

     J.J., (CHAD):

WAY OUT IN THE WATER (WHERE IS MY MIND)
SEE IT SWIMMIN' WHERE IS MY MIND (WHERE IS MY MIND)

     J.J.:

WHERE IS MY MIND?

     CHAD:

WITH YOUR FEET ON THE AIR AND YOUR HEAD ON THE GROUND
YEAH

     [***SET TRANSITION:*** *the set transforms back to RGB storefront.*
     CHAD and J.J. change back into their RGB uniforms]

     J.J.:

Your mind's somewhere tropical?

     CHAD:

Yeah, something like that. Where was your mind?

J.J.:

(not listening)
Okay. Well I'm sure you've got work to do somewhere else.
(waves her hand dismissively)

CHAD:

Oh…yeah, totally. Uh, yeah. Talk to you later then, I guess.

*[CHAD backs away from the checkout lane desk and exits
STAGE LEFT, walking past ROCK and AUGUST. Their dialogue is
now audible]*

My Curse

*[ROCK and AUGUST stand behind the customer service desk.
ROCK does all the talking, AUGUST the listening]*

[The red clock reads 1:22]

ROCK:

…and so we are looking at a reduction in returns by 2%. It's
super important we give the white glove treatment to every
customer and maybe we can help curb the return scorecard. Any
questions?

AUGUST:

You seem distracted. Is everything okay?

ROCK:

Yeah. No. I…I don't know.
(looks away)

AUGUST:

(concerned)
Whoa whoa, what's up?
(reaches out to touch his arm)

ROCK:

(recoils from her touch)
I have something to tell you. Swear to me you won't tell anyone.

AUGUST:

(whispers, breathless)
Anything.

ROCK:

There's talks of a reorganization. I hear they're going to
"right-size" RGB for some damn reason.
     (uses finger quotes at "right-size")

AUGUST:

     (annoyed)
Oh. That's all? They pull this crap every two years. Why worry?
You've survived the last…three, right?
     (counts on her fingers at the pause)

ROCK:

     (surprised)
Well, yeah. But this is retail! No one's safe when it comes to a
re-org.

AUGUST:

I'm sure you'll be fine, Rock. You're the best manager in this
dump!
     (reaches out to touch his arm again)

ROCK:

Yeah, but if my position is made "no longer available," I'll
lose my apartment at Windows Vista. We won't be neighbors
anymore.

     *(MANN enters from STAGE RIGHT. He points to ROCK and
     motions for him to come to him)*
Uh oh, this can't be good.
     *(moves away before AUGUST can touch his arm. He walks
     across the stage to MANN. MANN turns his back to the
     audience; ROCK faces the audience. Their dialogue is
     inaudible)*

AUGUST:

(sighs)

I WATCHED YOU WALK AWAY
HOPELESS, WITH NOTHING TO SAY
I STRAIN MY EYES
HOPING TO SEE YOU AGAIN

➔ SINGING (*whispering*)

THIS IS MY CURSE (THE LONGING)
THIS IS MY CURSE (TIME)
THIS IS MY CURSE (THE YEARNING)
THIS IS MY CURSE

THERE IS LOVE BURNING TO FIND YOU
WILL YOU WAIT FOR ME?
WILL YOU BE THERE?

YOUR SILENCE HAUNTS ME
BUT I STILL HUNGER FOR YOU

➔ SINGING   (*whispering*)

THIS IS MY CURSE (THE WANTING)
THIS IS MY CURSE (TIME)
THIS IS MY CURSE (THE NEEDING)
THIS IS MY CURSE

THERE IS LOVE BURNING TO FIND YOU
WILL YOU WAIT FOR ME?

AND STILL I WANT
AND STILL I ACHE
BUT STILL I WAIT
TO SEE YOU AGAIN

DYING, INSIDE, THESE WALLS
DYING, INSIDE, THESE WALLS

AND I SEE YOUR FACE IN THESE TEARS

IN THESE TEARS
AND I SEE YOUR FACE...

        *(ROCK finishes his talk with MANN. MANN exits STAGE RIGHT.
        ROCK is shaking his head as he returns to the customer
        service desk)*

THERE IS LOVE
THERE IS LOVE
THERE IS LOVE
THERE IS LOVE
        (singing begins to taper to a whisper)
There is love
There is love
There is love

        ROCK:

August.

        AUGUST:

        (looking at ROCK)
There is love.

        ROCK:

Wait, what?

        AUGUST:

        (stunned, embarrassed)
What? I-I didn't say anything.
        (changes subject)
What's up?

ROCK:

Um, okay.
        (*his voice changes, almost robotic*)
I have been reminded to tell you that touching of a manager by
an associate is strictly forbidden. It is against company policy
and can be a dismissible offense. Do you understand?

AUGUST:

What the hell? What's this all about?
        (*surprised anger*)

ROCK:
Your attempt to touch my arm earlier. Mr. Mann saw this and
intervened.

AUGUST:

Oh *Jesus*. That dude has eyes EVERYWHERE! Legend has it, he has
no home. He sleeps on a cot in the Performance Development Room.
Is that true?

ROCK:

When you're in a big box like this long enough, this place
becomes your home. Hell, this place is my home. And no, I'm sure
Mr. Mann has a home.
        (*laughing*)

AUGUST:

Rock, that's pretty depressing actually.

ROCK:

Yeah…it's sad once you hear yourself say it out loud…
        (*shakes his head*)
Back to business. Do you understand?

AUGUST:

That what, you and I can never have a relationship?

ROCK:

(surprised)
Relationship? When you can't even touch me, yeah. There's no relationship possible. Who said relationship?

AUGUST:

(stammers)
I-I could've sworn you did.
(recuperates)
Must get pretty lonely.

(CUSTOMER #6 enters from the entrance/exit. She has a product in her hand. She begins to walk towards the customer service desk)

ROCK:

It does indeed. You have a customer.
(points to CUSTOMER #6 and exits STAGE LEFT)

AUGUST:

Hello ma'am, welcome to Really Good Buy. How can I help you?

CUSTOMER #6:

Yeah, I'd like to return this.
(hands AUGUST the boxed product)

AUGUST:

Okay then. Do you have a receipt?

CUSTOMER #6:

Uh, no.

AUGUST:

(AUGUST looks towards the audience. She bows her head and speaks into the headset attached to her green polo shirt)

Hey Chad? I've got another one for you…

[SET TRANSITION: *The lights descend upon the stage, setting the stage dark]*

All My life

[BEGIN SCENE]

[**SET TRANSITION:** *Home theater department. Several flat screen televisions adorn television stands. A checkout lane is near STAGE RIGHT. It stands perpendicular to the 'wall' of televisions]*

(RICKY is standing at the checkout lane. He is facing the audience. He is visibly excited. EMPLOYEE #3 walks up to talk with him)

[The red clock reads 2:51]

EMPLOYEE #3

(waves)
Hey Ricky!

RICKY:

(does not look up from the computer monitor)
Hey……man.

EMPLOYEE #3:

Oh, did you forget my name? That's okay, it's-

RICKY:

(interrupts)
Employee number three, right?

EMPLOYEE #3:

(surprised)
N-no. Why would you say that? Is that because I was the third employee to walk up earlier?

RICKY:

(pauses)
Well……yeah.

EMPLOYEE #3:

Ah. That's fair. Well, my name's actually-

RICKY:

(interrupts)
Unimportant to the story. Do you……need something?

EMPLOYEE #3:

Oh nothing. The store's slow and I'm bored as hell. What're you
looking up?
(points to the computer monitor)

RICKY:

Employee number three, I'm going to let you in on a little
secret about retail. But not right now. Right now, I'm searching
for something.

EMPLOYEE #3:

What are you searching for?

RICKY:

(looks up from computer monitor)
ALL MY LIFE I'VE BEEN SEARCHING FOR SOMETHING
SOMETHING NEVER COMES NEVER LEADS TO NOTHING
NOTHING SATISFIES BUT I'M GETTING CLOSE
CLOSER TO THE PRIZE AT THE END OF THE ROPE
(steps away from the checkout lane)
ALL NIGHT LONG I DREAM OF THE DAY
WHEN IT COMES AROUND THEN IT'S TAKEN AWAY
LEAVES ME WITH THE FEELING THAT I FEEL THE MOST

FEEL IT COME TO LIFE WHEN I SEE YOUR GHOST

        EMPLOYEE #3:

What are you talking about?

        RICKY:

If there is one thing that is slightly better than clocking out
at the end of a shift, it's clocking for lunch. Want to help me
decide?
        EMPLOYEE #3:

I dunno, man. My lunch isn't for another hour.

        RICKY:

COME DOWN DON'T YOU RESIST
YOU HAVE SUCH A DELICATE WRIST
AND IF I GIVE IT A TWIST
SOMETHING TO HOLD WHEN I LOSE MY GRIP
WILL I FIND SOMETHING IN THERE
TO GIVE ME JUST WHAT I NEED?
ANOTHER REASON TO BLEED
ONE BY ONE HIDDEN UP MY SLEEVE
ONE BY ONE HIDDEN UP MY SLEEVE

        EMPLOYEE #3:

        (annoyed and startled)
Okay okay, fine! Um, Panda Express?

        RICKY:

HEY DON'T LET IT GO TO WASTE
I LOVE IT BUT I HATE THE TASTE
WEIGHT KEEPING ME DOWN
WEIGHT KEEPING ME DOWN

(EMPLOYEE #2 approaches from STAGE LEFT. He joins the conversation with EMPLOYEE #3 and RICKY. Their conversation supersedes RICKY'S singing)

RICKY:

(WILL I FIND A BELIEVER)
(ANOTHER ONE WHO BELIEVES)
(ANOTHER ONE TO DECEIVE)
(OVER AND OVER DOWN ON MY KNEES)
(IF I GET ANY CLOSER)
(AND IF YOU OPEN UP WIDE)
(AND IF YOU LET ME INSIDE)
(ON AND ON I'VE GOT NOTHING TO HIDE)
(ON AND ON I'VE GOT NOTHING TO HIDE)

EMPLOYEE #2:

(speaking to EMPLOYEE #3)
Hey, what's he singing out?

EMPLOYEE #3:

What to eat, apparently.

EMPLOYEE #2:

Oh, that's a decision not to be taken lightly.
(to RICKY)
How about McDonald's?

RICKY:

HEY DON'T LET IT GO TO WASTE
I LOVE IT BUT I HATE THE TASTE
WEIGHT KEEPING ME DOWN
WEIGHT KEEPING ME DOWN
(returns to the checkout lane computer)
ALL MY LIFE I'VE BEEN SEARCHING FOR SOMETHING
SOMETHING NEVER COMES NEVER LEADS TO NOTHING
NOTHING SATISFIES BUT I'M GETTING CLOSE
CLOSER TO THE PRIZE AT THE END OF THE ROPE

EMPLOYEE #3:

(to EMPLOYEE #2)
I think he's looking up on Google Maps what's close by.
(EMPLOYEE #2 nods in agreement)

RICKY:

ALL NIGHT LONG I DREAM OF THE DAY
WHEN IT COMES AROUND, WHEN IT'S TAKEN AWAY
LEAVES ME WITH THE FEELING THAT I FEEL THE MOST
FEEL IT COME TO LIFE WHEN I SEE YOUR GHOST

EMPLOYEE #3:

Qdoba?

RICKY:

(shakes head)
AND I'M DONE, DONE AND I'M ON TO THE NEXT ONE

EMPLOYEE #2:

Subway?

RICKY:

(shakes head)
AND I'M DONE, DONE AND I'M ON TO THE NEXT ONE

EMPLOYEE #3:

Smashburger?

RICKY:

(shakes head)
AND I'M DONE, DONE AND I'M ON TO THE NEXT ONE

EMPLOYEE #2:

Noodles and Company?

RICKY:

(shakes head)
AND I'M DONE, DONE AND I'M ON TO THE NEXT ONE

EMPLOYEE #3:

(snaps fingers)
Chick-Fil-A.

*(EMPLOYEE #2 and 3 list off four more restaurants to which
RICKY agrees to none)*

RICKY:

AND I'M DONE, DONE AND I'M ON TO THE NEXT ONE
AND I'M DONE, DONE AND I'M ON TO THE NEXT ONE
AND I'M DONE, DONE AND I'M ON TO THE NEXT ONE
AND I'M DONE, DONE AND I'M ON TO THE NEXT ONE!

*(AUGUST enters from STAGE LEFT to STAGE RIGHT. She
does not engage or look at the three employees as she
walks by. This stops RICKY'S singing instantly)*

EMPLOYEE #2:

I guess we know where Ricky's mind is.
(nudges EMPLOYEE #3 in the ribs)

RICKY:

(shouting)

Hey hey there bay-bay. Goin' my way?
        *(a smug smirk appears on his face as he watches her walk
        from behind)*

        AUGUST:

Eat shit and die, Ricky.
        (exits STAGE RIGHT)

        EMPLOYEE #3:

I-I don't think she likes you very much.

        RICKY:

Nah man, she's kidding. That's……that's how we flirt. Screw it,
I'm just going to get something from the snack wall. I'm on
lunch, bitches! See you in thirty!
        (flashes a peace sign before exiting STAGE RIGHT)

        EMPLOYEE #3:

He's kind of a douche, isn't he?

        EMPLOYEE #2:

Uh, yeah. Comes with the territory. When you're the best
salesman in three states, it goes straight to your head. Gotta
love retail. It gets to you after a while. Come on, I see some
customers walk into our department.
        (EMPLOYEE #2 and #3 exit STAGE LEFT)

        [END SCENE]

Scream with me

[**SET TRANSITION:** *The break room. There are a random
assortment of mismatched chairs and small tables. A small
TV hangs on the wall playing a movie. There is a small
counter with a sink, paper tower dispenser, etc. and a
tall, battered refrigerator. There is a small battered
couch. The room is painted taupe with green stripes, highly
unflattering*]

[*GEORGE ATKINS sits at one of the tables on a broken chair.
He is eating fried chicken, mashed potatoes. He has a paper
napkin tucked into his green polo and a book in his hand.
EMPLOYEE #1 sits on the couch and watching the movie.
AUGUST WINTERS enters the break room from STAGE LEFT. She
is frustrated}*

[*The red clock reads 3:05*]

AUGUST:

   (*slams break room door and snorts angrily*)
Ugh!

GEORGE:

   (*without looking up from his book*)
Hey there August

AUGUST:

   (*snorts angrily*)
Ugh! Why the hell do I still work in retail? I should've stayed
in school!

EMPLOYEE #1:

   (*looks away from the TV*)
You were in school? Why'd you drop out?

GEORGE:

I was in school. Graduated, too. 35 years later, I'm still doing
retail. School doesn't do shit for you.
     (turns the page in his book)
AUGUST:

     (ignores GEORGE)
I dropped out because, well, at the time I was making good
money. Not here, obviously, somewhere else. But I decided to
move to Colorado because of a boy. Let me tell you how well *that*
worked out! Now I'm stuck here because it's the only thing out
here. All I do is deal with stupid returns and exchanges!
     (crosses her arms)

GEORGE:

No, no, tell us how you really feel.
     (turns another page)

AUGUST:

EVER FEEL LIKE DYING,
EVER FEEL ALONE,
EVER FEEL LIKE CRYING,
     (pauses and places her hand on her headset)

VOICE ON RADIO:

Code Adam! We have a Code Adam! Lost child!

AUGUST:

LOST CHILD IN A STORE,
     (throws her headset and walkie talkie on the table)
EVER FEEL LIFE PUSHING,
SHOVING YOU AWAY,
EVER FEEL LIKE BREAKING DOWN,
FUNERAL IN THE RAIN
FEEL LIKE SLIPPING AWAY,
     (walks over to the corner near EMPLOYEE #1)
     (screams)

STAND IN THE CORNER AND SCREAM WITH ME,
A BODY FULL OF EMPTY,
A HEAD THATS FULL OF RAGE,
BETTER BELIEVE IT,
STAND IN THE CLOSET AND SCREAM WITH ME
A MIND THATS LIKE A FIRE,
DRIVIN BY THE PAIN,
BETTER BELIEVE IT

  EMPLOYEE #1:

  (surprised)
Jesus!

  AUGUST:

  (ignoring EMPLOYEE #1, walks away from the corner)
EVER FEEL LIKE LYING,
DOWN INSIDE A GRAVE,
LISTEN TO THE EULOGY,
A BUYER OF THE HATE,

  GEORGE:

No, can't say that I have…
  (flips another page)

  AUGUST:

EVER DANCE BESIDE THE DEVIL,
TASTE THE BARREL OF A GUAGE,
  (turns her fingers into a gun and places it into her mouth)

EVER PULL THE TRIGGER,
  (pulls the trigger on her "gun")
THE LIGHT BEGINS TO FADE,
FEEL LIKE SLIPPING AWAY
  (walks towards a chair but does not sit)
STAND IN THE CORNER AND SCREAM WITH ME,
A BODY FULL OF EMPTY,
A HEAD THAT'S FULL OF RAGE,
BETTER BELIEVE IT,
STAND IN THE CLOSET AND SCREAM WITH ME

A MIND THAT'S LIKE A FIRE,
DRIVIN' BY THE PAIN,
BETTER BELIEVE IT
      (sinks into the chair)
I'VE ASKED YOU FOR FORGIVENESS,
I'VE ASKED YOU FOR YOUR GRACE,
I'VE ASKED YOU FOR YOUR BLESSING,
I'VE ASKED THAT I BE SAVED,

STAND IN THE CORNER AND SCREAM WITH ME,
A BODY FULL OF EMPTY,
A HEAD THAT'S FULL OF RAGE,
BETTER BELIEVE IT,
      (sighs heavily)

      (The break room door opens. ROCK pokes his head in the door
      and looks around)

      ROCK:

Break time's over, boys! Time to get back to work!

      GEORGE:

      (finishes his meal and closes his book)
It's probably best. August's having a break down over here.

      (EMPLOYEE #1 leaves first, gently walking past ROCK as he
      passes through the door)

      AUGUST:

      (snaps)
Shut up George.

      GEORGE:

      (before leaving, thumbs towards AUGUST to ROCK)
See what I mean?

      (both men leave. RICKY enters the break room and closes the
      door)

AUGUST:

(*looking up from her chair and whispers audibly*)
Ah *shit.*

Tainted love

RICKY:

Hey hey there beautiful.
    (smirks smugly)

AUGUST:

(says nothing)

RICKY:

Aw, the cold shoulder? Already? After everything we've been
through last night?
    (attempts to put his arm around AUGUST's shoulder)

AUGUST:

Last night was a drunken mistake, Ricky.
    (shirks RICKY's arm)

RICKY:

Oh yeah? And the night before that? And before that? And before
that?
    (crosses his arms)

AUGUST:

……yes……

RICKY:

Aw, come on baby! You know you're beautiful. I wish you weren't
but dammit all, you just are!

AUGUST:

That is…the lamest and weirdest compliment I've ever gotten.

        RICKY:

Thanks!

        AUGUST:
That wasn't a compliment, Ricky. All this is,
        (sweeps her arm all over RICKY)
this is tainted love.

        RICKY:

Aw, baby, come on! Don't say that!
        (attempts to wrap his arm around her neck)

        AUGUST:

        (violently shoves his arm away and stands)

        *[RICKY and AUGUST begin a sequence of embrace and rejection
        by AUGUST to RICKY. It prevails until the end of the song,
        all sung by AUGUST]*

SOMETIMES I FEEL I'VE GOT TO
RUN AWAY I'VE GOT TO
GET AWAY
FROM THE PAIN THAT YOU DRIVE INTO THE HEART OF ME
THE LOVE WE SHARE
SEEMS TO GO NOWHERE
I'VE LOST MY LIGHTS
I TOSS AND TURN I CAN'T SLEEP AT NIGHT

ONCE I RAN TO YOU (I RAN)
NOW I'LL RUN FROM YOU
THIS TAINTED LOVE YOU'VE GIVEN
I GIVE YOU ALL A GIRL COULD GIVE YOU
TAKE MY TEARS AND THAT'S NOT NEARLY ALL
TAINTED LOVE
TAINTED LOVE

NOW I KNOW I'VE GOT TO
RUN AWAY I'VE GOT TO
GET AWAY

YOU DON'T REALLY WANT ANY MORE FROM ME
TO MAKE THINGS RIGHT
YOU NEED SOMEONE TO HOLD YOU TIGHT
YOU THINK LOVE IS TO PRAY
I'M SORRY I DON'T PRAY THAT WAY

    RICKY:

ONCE I RAN TO YOU (I RAN)
NOW I'LL RUN FROM YOU
THIS TAINTED LOVE YOU'VE GIVEN
I GIVE YOU ALL A BOY COULD GIVE YOU
TAKE MY TEARS AND THAT'S NOT NEARLY ALL
TAINTED LOVE
TAINTED LOVE

    (RICKY begins to saunter up to AUGUST, a smug smile on his face)

    AUGUST:

DON'T TOUCH ME PLEASE
I CANNOT STAND THE WAY YOU TEASE
I LOVE YOU THOUGH YOU HURT ME SO
NOW I'M GOING TO PACK MY THINGS AND GO
TOUCH ME BABY, TAINTED LOVE
TOUCH ME BABY, TAINTED LOVE
TOUCH ME BABY, TAINTED LOVE

ONCE I RAN TO YOU (I RAN)
NOW I'LL RUN FROM YOU
THIS TAINTED LOVE YOU'VE GIVEN
I GIVE YOU ALL A GIRL COULD GIVE YOU
TAKE MY TEARS AND THAT'S NOT NEARLY ALL
TAINTED LOVE
TAINTED LOVE
TAINTED LOVE

    (RICKY makes one final move and forces a kiss on AUGUST's lips. She initially resists but eventually gives in to his kiss. They embrace)

[LLEWELLYN and J.J. open the door to the break room and are talking, inaudible. They stop talking when they see RICKY and AUGUST kissing and hugging. LLEWELLYN is visibly distraught; J.J. is in shock. They both back away and close the door quietly. RICKY and AUGUST do not notice them standing there]

[LIGHTS FADE, CURTAIN DROPS. INTERMISSION]

<u>INTERMISSION!</u>

ACT 2

Call Me When Your Sober

[BEGIN SCENE]

[**SET TRANSITION**: *WINDOWS VISTA APARTMENTS, AUGUST's
bedroom. The room is still disheveled from earlier. The bed
is tucked into the corner near STAGE LEFT of the bedroom.
AUGUST lays on her bed still in her Really Good Buy
uniform. She is alone in her room and texting on her phone]*

[The red clock reads 8:09]

*[STAGE LEFT is RICKY. He is looking down at his phone and
'texting' AUGUST. He has a little bit of a drunken swagger
to him as he stands and texts. A spotlight illuminates him
standing there and only the audience can tell he is
standing STAGE LEFT. He is animated as he sends and
receives texts from AUGUST]*

AUGUST:

     (reading)
Hey hey hey baby.
     (looks up)
Oh goodie. He's drunk already.
     (looks down and texts back)
     (pause)
     (reading)
Nah baby, I not drunk!
     (looks up and asks the audience)
Is it back I can practically hear him slurring his words?
     (looks down and texts back)
     (pause)
     [The phone begins to ring]
Ah shit.
     (answers the phone)
What.

(A voice answers on the other end. The voice is broadcast
throughout the theater)

VOICE [RICKY]:

(slightly slurring his words)
Hey baby

AUGUST:

What do you want?

VOICE [RICKY]:

Whoa whoa, what's with the attitude?

AUGUST:

(annoyed)
Ricky, what do you want? I've had a long day and you sneaking up
on me earlier didn't help.

VOICE [RICKY]:

(shocked)
Aw come on, you know you liked it. That's what people who are in
love do, you know.

AUGUST:

(sits up on her bed)
DON'T CRY TO ME.
IF YOU LOVED ME,
YOU WOULD BE HERE WITH ME.
YOU WANT ME,
COME FIND ME.
MAKE UP YOUR MIND.

VOICE [RICKY]:

What, come over now? But...the club...

        AUGUST:

            (ignores him and continues)
SHOULD I LET YOU FALL?
LOSE IT ALL?
SO MAYBE YOU CAN REMEMBER YOURSELF.
CAN'T KEEP BELIEVING,
WE'RE ONLY DECEIVING OURSELVES .
AND I'M SICK OF THE LIE,
AND YOU'RE TOO LATE.

DON'T CRY TO ME.
IF YOU LOVED ME,
YOU WOULD BE HERE WITH ME.
YOU WANT ME,
COME FIND ME.
MAKE UP YOUR MIND.

COULDN'T TAKE THE BLAME.
SICK WITH SHAME.
MUST BE EXHAUSTING TO LOSE YOUR OWN GAME.
SELFISHLY HATED,
NO WONDER YOU'RE JADED.
YOU CAN'T PLAY THE VICTIM THIS TIME,
AND YOU'RE TOO LATE.

DON'T CRY TO ME.
IF YOU LOVED ME,
YOU WOULD BE HERE WITH ME.
YOU WANT ME,
COME FIND ME.
MAKE UP YOUR MIND.

YOU NEVER CALL ME WHEN YOU'RE SOBER.
YOU ONLY WANT IT CAUSE IT'S OVER,
IT'S OVER.

        VOICE [RICKY]:

Girl, I call you plenty when I'm sober!

AUGUST:

HOW COULD I HAVE BURNED PARADISE?
HOW COULD I - YOU WERE NEVER MINE.

SO DON'T CRY TO ME.
IF YOU LOVED ME,
YOU WOULD BE HERE WITH ME.
DON'T LIE TO ME,
JUST GET YOUR THINGS.
I'VE MADE UP YOUR MIND.

VOICE [RICKY]:

You've made up my mind, huh? Well, my mind says your ass belongs
on the dance floor!

AUGUST:

Really? That's all you've got for me? Ass on the dance floor?
Where are you anyways?

VOICE [RICKY]:

Pre-gaming at my apartment.

AUGUST:

Are you alone?

VOICE [RICKY]:

(excited)
Yes!

AUGUST:

Easy tiger, I'm not coming over. I just wanted you to realize
how pathetic you are for drinking alone.

RICKY:

Ouch, baby. Such ouch. You blew me over like au-*gust* of wind.
   (laughing)

AUGUST:

(begins to smile then looks up and notices the audience. The smile disappears before she responds)

God, you're such a dork.
   (pauses)
What time are you going?

VOICE [RICKY]:

(excited)
Yes! I'm getting ready right now! I'll see you there soon!

(a loud click is audible. AUGUST tosses the phone on the bed)

AUGUST:

God, I hate him so much.
   (pauses)
Maybe I should invite J.J.
   (runs her hands through her hair)
Nah, she'll never accept. She's too absorbed in her reading.. On the other hand, it'll do her some good to get some fresh air…
   (turns towards STAGE LEFT and raises her fist to pound on the wall)

[**SET TRANSITION:** *The lighting focused on her room drops out completely before she knocks. A new set of lighting illuminates J.J.'s room LEFT adjacent to AUGUST's room. She is reading a book]*

All the love in the world

[***SET TRANSITION:*** *J.J.'s bed is nestled in the corner near STAGE RIGHT. Her bedroom is neat and tidy, the complete opposite of AUGUST's bedroom]*

[The red clock rewinds to 8:06]

J.J.:

WATCHING ALL THE INSECTS MARCH ALONG
SEEM TO KNOW JUST RIGHT WHERE THEY BELONG
SMEARS OF FACE REFLECTING IN THE CHROME
HIDING IN THE CROWD I'M ALL ALONE
     (turns a page in her book)
NO ONE'S HEARD A SINGLE WORD I'VE SAID
THEY DON'T SOUND AS GOOD OUTSIDE MY HEAD
IT LOOKS AS THOUGH THE PAST IS HERE TO STAY
I'VE BECOME A MILLION MILES A...
     (looks up)
WHY DO YOU GET ALL THE LOVE IN THE WORLD?
     (looks left towards AUGUST's room through the wall)
WHY DO YOU GET ALL THE LOVE IN THE WORLD?
     (shakes her head)
ALL THE JAGGED EDGES DISAPPEAR
COLORS ALL LOOK BRIGHTER WHEN YOU'RE NEAR
THE STARS ARE ALL AFIRE IN THE SKY
SOMETIMES I GET SO LONELY I COULD...

[pounding on the wall, coming from AUGUST's room]

AUGUST:

(shouting)
Hey bitch, I'm going to the club. You should come!

J.J.:

WHY DO YOU GET ALL THE LOVE IN THE WORLD?

AUGUST:

(shouting)
What? Ugh, never mind! Don't wait up for me!

J.J.

WHY DO YOU GET ALL THE LOVE IN THE WORLD?
WHY DO YOU GET ALL THE LOVE IN THE WORLD?
WHY DO YOU GET ALL THE LOVE IN THE WORLD?
WHY DO YOU GET ALL THE LOVE IN THE WORLD?
WHY DO YOU GET ALL THE LOVE IN THE WORLD?
WHY DO YOU GET ALL THE LOVE IN THE WORLD?
WHY DO YOU GET ALL THE LOVE IN THE WORLD?
WHY DO YOU GET ALL THE LOVE IN THE WORLD?
*(stands from her bed and slowly walks around her room until
she comes full circle to her bed but does not sit back
down)*

WHY DO YOU GET ALL THE LOVE IN THE WORLD?
WHY DO YOU GET ALL THE LOVE IN THE WORLD?
WHY DO YOU GET ALL THE LOVE IN THE WORLD?
WHY DO YOU GET ALL THE LOVE IN THE WORLD?
WHY DO YOU GET ALL THE LOVE IN THE WORLD?
*(kneels down and reaches underneath the bed, searching for
something)*

WHY DO YOU GET ALL THE LOVE IN THE WORLD?
WHY DO YOU GET ALL THE LOVE IN THE WORLD?
WHY DO YOU GET ALL THE LOVE IN THE WORLD?
WHY DO YOU GET ALL THE LOVE IN THE WORLD?
Why do you get all the love in the world?
*(she finds what she's looking for, a large red bag.
The red bag mentioned by AUGUST earlier)*

WHY DO YOU GET ALL THE LOVE?
WHY DO YOU GET ALL THE LOVE?
WHY DO YOU GET ALL THE LOVE?
*(she slowly pulls an outfit from the red bag. Piece after
piece comes out of the bag with a pair of shiny heels
finalizing the end of her withdrawal)*
WHY DO YOU GET ALL THE LOVE?
WHY DO YOU GET ALL THE LOVE?

WHY DO YOU GET ALL THE LOVE?
    *(she looks at the audience as she holds up her outfit,
    a particularly liberal skirt with a low-cut top)*
WHY DO YOU GET ALL THE LOVE?
    (smiling)
I'll see you there……*bitch*.

    [SET TRANSITION: *The light descend, setting the stage to be
    dark]*

Get Lucky

[**SET TRANSITION:** *A spotlight illuminates the bathroom. RICKY is in the bathroom. It is a spotless bathroom with bottles of cologne surrounding the sink. A large half-mirror facing STAGE RIGHT is in the bathroom]*

(RICKY is shirtless in front of a mirror. The audience sees a tattoo of wings on his back. He is flexing in the mirror before he begins to sing. He dresses himself in typical club attire. It is obvious RICKY is getting ready for a night at the MACINTOSH CLUB)

[The red clock reads 8:12]

RICKY:

LIKE THE LEGEND OF THE PHOENIX
ALL ENDS WITH BEGINNINGS
WHAT KEEPS THE PLANET SPINNING, UH
THE FORCE OF LOVE BEGINNING, LOOK

(RICKY runs his hands through his hair before pointing his fingers like guns at himself in the mirror)

WE'VE COME TOO FAR TO GIVE UP WHO WE ARE
SO LET'S RAISE THE BAR AND OUR CUPS TO THE STARS

(RICKY sprays on some cologne and puts on his shirt)

SHE'S UP ALL NIGHT 'TIL THE SUN
I'M UP ALL NIGHT TO GET SOME
SHE'S UP ALL NIGHT FOR GOOD FUN
I'M UP ALL NIGHT TO GET LUCKY

(He puts on his pants, all the while grinding his hips)

WE'RE UP ALL NIGHT 'TIL THE SUN
WE'RE UP ALL NIGHT TO GET SOME
WE'RE UP ALL NIGHT FOR GOOD FUN

WE'RE UP ALL NIGHT TO GET LUCKY

    (*RICKY turns to face the audience. There is a smug smile on HIS face. He continues to sing*)

WE'RE UP ALL NIGHT TO GET LUCKY
WE'RE UP ALL NIGHT TO GET LUCKY
WE'RE UP ALL NIGHT TO GET LUCKY
WE'RE UP ALL NIGHT TO GET LUCKY

(RICKY departs through the "bathroom door" facing the audience then exits STAGE LEFT)

[**SET TRANSITION**: *Spotlight fades on RICKY and the BATHROOM. A different spotlight illuminates a BEDROOM. The BEDROOM set is adjacent to the BATHROOM. The BEDROOM is not attached to the BATHROOM; a one foot should be in place to show THEY do not live together*]

[*Enter AUGUST WINTERS. She is in the bedroom. She is lying on her bed before begins to sing. She is clad in black undergarments. It is apparent that she is getting ready for the evening as well*]

AUGUST:

    (*Playing with a purple ribbon*)
THE PRESENT HAS NO RIBBON
YOUR GIFT KEEPS ON GIVING,
WHAT IS THIS I'M FEELING?
IF YOU WANNA LEAVE I'M READY (AH)

    (*AUGUST gets up from her bed and dances towards her closet for some clothes. She starts to dress in a purple sundress. She continues to sing*)

WE'VE COME TOO FAR TO GIVE UP WHO WE ARE
SO LETS RAISE THE BAR AND OUR CUPS TO THE STARS

    (*She spray on some perfume, onto her neck and her wrists*)

HE'S UP ALL NIGHT 'TIL THE SUN
I'M UP ALL NIGHT TO GET SOME
HE'S UP ALL NIGHT FOR GOOD FUN
I'M UP ALL NIGHT TO GET LUCKY

(She ties her hair back with the purple ribbon)

WE'RE UP ALL NIGHT 'TIL THE SUN
WE'RE UP ALL NIGHT TO GET SOME
WE'RE UP ALL NIGHT FOR GOOD FUN
WE'RE UP ALL NIGHT TO GET LUCKY

(AUGUST turns to face the audience once she is fully dressed)

WE'RE UP ALL NIGHT TO GET LUCKY
WE'RE UP ALL NIGHT TO GET LUCKY
WE'RE UP ALL NIGHT TO GET LUCKY
WE'RE UP ALL NIGHT TO GET LUCKY
(Cups her hand around her mouth and blows a kiss to the audience)

[AUGUST leaves via the "door" facing the audience and exits STAGE RIGHT]

[**SET TRANSITION:** *Spotlight fades on AUGUST and HER bedroom. The bedroom and bathroom break away from each other as the song is played. Once the bedroom and bathroom are moved, stage lights will rise to reveal the interior of the Macintosh Club. There are several tall cocktail tables with matching chairs near STAGE RIGHT and LEFT. A small dance floor is in the middle, in front of the bar. The bar is slightly angled, facing slightly towards STAGE LEFT. The entrance is at STAGE LEFT. The bathroom hallway door is at STAGE RIGHT. A few people are already inside with a bartender and a waitress happily serving]*

(PONY is standing behind the bar. He is serving drinks as each person comes up and asks for one)

PONY:

WE'RE UP ALL NIGHT TO GET
WE'RE UP ALL NIGHT TO GET
WE'RE UP ALL NIGHT TO GET
WE'RE UP ALL NIGHT TO GET

WE'RE UP ALL NIGHT TO GET
TOGETHER
WE'RE UP ALL NIGHT TO GET
LET'S GET FUNKED AGAIN
WE'RE UP ALL NIGHT TO GET FUNKY
WE'RE UP ALL NIGHT TO GET LUCKY

WE'RE UP ALL NIGHT TO GET LUCKY
WE'RE UP ALL NIGHT TO GET LUCKY
WE'RE UP ALL NIGHT TO GET LUCKY
WE'RE UP ALL NIGHT TO GET LUCKY

WE'RE UP ALL NIGHT TO GET LUCKY
WE'RE UP ALL NIGHT TO GET LUCKY
WE'RE UP ALL NIGHT TO GET LUCKY
WE'RE UP ALL NIGHT TO GET LUCKY

[Enter VIQI. As PONY prepares drinks, she grabs them and places them on her tray. She continues to sing]

VIQI (PONY):

WE'VE (WE'RE UP ALL NIGHT TO GET LUCKY)
COME TOO FAR (WE'RE UP ALL NIGHT TO GET LUCKY)
TO GIVE UP (WE'RE UP ALL NIGHT TO GET LUCKY)
WHO WE ARE (WE'RE UP ALL NIGHT TO GET LUCKY)
SO LET'S (WE'RE UP ALL NIGHT TO GET LUCKY)
RAISE THE BAR (WE'RE UP ALL NIGHT TO GET LUCKY)
AND OUR CUPS (WE'RE UP ALL NIGHT TO GET LUCKY)
TO THE STARS (WE'RE UP ALL NIGHT TO GET LUCKY)

VIQI:

(raises her tray full of empty glasses up)
SHE'S UP ALL NIGHT 'TIL THE SUN
I'M UP ALL NIGHT TO GET SOME
HE'S UP ALL NIGHT FOR GOOD FUN
I'M UP ALL NIGHT TO GET LUCKY

(VIQI returns back behind the bar and gives PONY a kiss and a wink towards the audience)

[ROCK and CHAD enter together through the front entrance via STAGE LEFT. They are wearing jeans and matching plaid button down shirts. They take a seat at a cocktail table and notice LLEWELLYN sitting at the bar. He is wearing cowboy boots, jeans, and a plain white t-shirt. LLEWELLYN does not notice ROCK and CHAD. LLEWELLYN is inebriated]

The End

(VIQI walks over to the table and takes their drink order. Their order is inaudible. VIQI walks away, CHAD takes notice of AUGUST)

[The red clock reads 9:00. From this point forward, the clock will read real time until the end of the musical]

CHAD:

(sits down at a cocktail table across from AUGUST)
Holy shit, look at August! She cleans up pretty good, huh?
(winks at ROCK)

ROCK:

Yeah…she really does.
(looks at LLEWELLYN)
Jesus, Lew's drunker than usual. I wonder what's up with him. Ricky's here too.

CHAD:

(ignores ROCK's question)
That's the funny thing about uniforms. You never know what anyone's hiding underneath that uni, guy or gal.

ROCK:

True story

CHAD:

So, why do you never ask out any of the girls? Especially August. I hear she's got a thing for you.

ROCK:

It's against company policy, Chad.

CHAD:

Oh, fuck policy. Who cares? You and the Mann are the only ones, that's who! You're the one always saying that when you're with the right woman, you're always home regardless of where you are!

ROCK:

Yeah, well while that's true, I don't see you asking out J.J. any time soon!
     (VIQI delivers two yellow drinks in a martini glass. ROCK points to the glass in question)
What the hell is this?

CHAD:

     (scoffs)
I would if she were here!
     (looks at the glasses)
It's a lemon drop! Pretty tasty.
     (He takes a glass and takes a sip)

     (J.J. enters from the entrance, STAGE LEFT. She is wearing a tight skirt with a matching shirt, complete with high heels. Everyone in the club stops to look at her as she crosses the dance floor to sit with AUGUST. Everyone reacts with surprise as she walks)

ROCK:

We need to talk about revoking your man card.
     (notices J.J. walking by)
Speak of the devil…

CHAD:

     (his jaw drops as he watched J.J.)
And she shall appear. Holy crap!

ROCK:

Man up! Let the street lights be your guide home!

CHAD:

Yeah, well. I ask out mine, you ask out yours. Deal?
(finishes his drink)

ROCK:

(sighs)
I don't know man. You go first.

(CHAD nervously leaves the table to walk towards J.J. and AUGUST's table but turns around, back to his table. ROCK attempts to shoo him away but CHAD fails to launch and sits back down)

ROCK:

(stands up and adjust his pants before sitting down)
I DON'T WANT THE STREET LIGHTS
LAUGHING AT THE GRAVE
HE SWEARS HE'S GONNA GIVE IT UP
IT'S NEVER GONNA BE ENOUGH

I JUST WANNA BE THERE
WHEN YOU'RE ALL ALONE
THINKING ABOUT A BETTER DAY
WHEN YOU HAD IT IN YOUR BONES

THIS COULD BE THE END
THIS COULD BE THE END
THIS COULD BE THE END
THIS COULD BE THE END
(looks towards AUGUST and hopes to catch her eye)
I SEE YOU IN THE EVENING
SITTING ON YOUR THRONE
YOU'RE PLAYING WITH A FIREBALL
AND POST IT UP AGAINST WALL
(hesitates to stand up)

I JUST WANNA HOLD YOU
TAKE YOU BY YOUR HAND
AND TELL YOU THAT YOU'RE GOOD ENOUGH
AND TELL YOU THAT IT'S GONNA BE TOUGH

THIS COULD BE THE END
THIS COULD BE THE END
THIS COULD BE THE END
THIS COULD BE THE END

COS I AIN'T GOT A HOME

RUNNING FROM THE STREET LIGHTS
SHINING ON THE GRAVE
ONCE YOU'VE HAD THE GOOD STUFF
NEVER GONNA FILL YOU UP

I WANNA BE THE ONE WHO
GIVES THEM ALL A WHIRL
AND GIVES THEM ALL THE FINGER AT IT
JUST A LITTLE TASTE OF IT

THIS COULD BE THE END
THIS COULD BE THE END
THIS COULD BE THE END
THIS COULD BE THE END

*[ROCK begins to realize that he needs to share his feelings
with AUGUST]*

COS I AIN'T GOT A HOME
I'LL FOREVER ROAM
NO I AIN'T GOT A HOME
I'LL FOREVER ROAM
(wrings his hands)
SAID I AIN'T GOT A HOME
I'LL FOREVER ROAM
NO I AIN'T GOT A HOME
I'LL FOREVER ROAM

I AIN'T GOT A HOME

CHAD:

So does this mean you'll do it?

ROCK:

(pauses)
Yeah man, I'll do it. I need a home and not just the Buy or
Vista.

CHAD:

Alright, man! Let's do this!

ROCK:

You first. That was the deal.

CHAD:

Pussy!
*(stands up and walks over to J.J. and AUGUST. Their
conversation is inaudible for now)*

*[The conversation focus switches to RICKY and PONY. RICKY
is sitting at the bar]*

Breaking the Girl

RICKY:

I just don't get it Pony. First she's hot towards me, then she's
a cold fish. Man, you shoulda seen her this afternoon. Couldn't
keep her hands offa me. Now look at her. Pretending I don't even
exist!
*(points towards AUGUST and J.J. sitting at the table near
STAGE RIGHT)*

PONY:

(cleaning a glass)
Maybe she thinks you think of her as a piece of meat, not a
woman.

RICKY:

Whoa, what? I don' treat her like a piece of meat!

PONY:

Look sonny, I saw the way you treated her last night. You can't
treat women like that.

RICKY:

What the hell do you know?
(takes a sip of his beer)

PONY:

I AM A MAN
CUT FROM THE KNOW
RARELY DO FRIENDS
COME AND THEN GO
SHE WAS A GIRL
SOFT BUT ESTRANGED
WE WERE THE TWO
OUR LIVES REARRANGED

FEELING SO GOOD THAT DAY
A FEELING OF LOVE THAT DAY

TWISTING AND TURNING
YOUR FEELINGS ARE BURNING
YOU'RE BREAKING THE GIRL
SHE MEANT YOU NO HARM
THINK YOU'RE SO CLEVER
BUT NOW YOU MUST SEVER
YOU'RE BREAKING THE GIRL
HE LOVES NO ONE ELSE

    (VIQI returns from serving drinks from the various patrons in the bar. She gives a kiss on PONY's cheek before she sings)

    VIQI:

RAISED BY MY DAD
GIRL OF THE DAY
HE WAS MY MAN
THAT WAS THE WAY
I WAS THE GIRL
LEFT ALONE
FEELING THE NEED
TO MAKE ME HER HOME
I DON'T KNOW WHAT, WHEN, OR WHY
THE TWILIGHT OF LOVE HAD ARRIVED

TWISTING AND TURNING
YOUR FEELINGS ARE BURNING
YOU'RE BREAKING THE GIRL
SHE MEANT YOU NO HARM
THINK YOU'RE SO CLEVER
BUT NOW YOU MUST SEVER
YOU'RE BREAKING THE GIRL
HE LOVES NO ONE ELSE

    PONY:

I know because I pulled that shit with Viqi here. I should've known better. Viqi here forgave me and she's the best thing that's ever happened to me since!

RICKY:

(raises eyebrows)
Really?

PONY:

See, I can't tell if you're being an asshole right now or not.

RICKY:

(stammers)
No, no! Not being an asshole, I swear!

PONY:

Good. Now go and tell her how beautiful she looks!

*(moves away to serve LLEWELLYN another drink and continues
to clean some barware. RICKY turns on his barstool and
looks at J.J. and AUGUST to see CHAD talking to them. He
waits until CHAD leaves)*

Oil and Water

Chad:

(wrings his hands)
Hey hey, J.J.!

J.J.

(ignores CHAD)
Ugh, I can't wait to dance tonight!

AUGUST:

What, you're going to boogie?

CHAD:

Hey August.

J.J.:

Uh, yeah! Duh?

AUGUST:

Hey Chad.

CHAD:

What're you talking about? You look amazing by the way, J.J.

J.J.:

(looking away)
Oh, hi Chad. When did you get here?

CHAD:

I've……been here a while.

        AUGUST:

Ouch.

        CHAD:

So hey, uh, J.J. I was wondering something.

        J.J.:

        (whispers loudly)
Ah shit, here it comes…

        CHAD:

You, uh, wanna go out sometime?

        J.J.:

        (pauses)
How do I put this nicely?
        (clears throat)
YOU AND I ARE LIKE OIL AND WATER
AND WE'VE BEEN TRYING, TRYING TRYING
OHHHH, TO MIX IT UP.
WE'VE BEEN DANCING ON A VOLCANO
AND WE'VE BEEN CRYING, CRYING, CRYING
OVER BLACKENED SOULS.
BABE, THIS WOULDN'T BE THE FIRST TIME,
IT WILL NOT BE THE LAST TIME.
THERE IS NO PARASOL THAT WOULD SHELTER THIS WEATHER.
I BEEN SMILING WITH ANCHORS ON MY SHOULDERS
BUT I'VE BEEN DYING, DYING, DYING
OHH, OHH, OH TO LET THEM GO.
BABE, THIS WOULDN'T BE THE FIRST TIME,
IT WILL NOT BE THE LAST TIME.
THERE IS NO PARASOL THAT WOULD SHELTER THIS WEATHER.
BABE, THIS WOULDN'T BE THE FIRST TIME,
IT WILL NOT BE THE LAST TIME.
WE WERE TRYING TO BELIEVE THAT EVERYTHING WOULD GET BETTER.
WE'VE BEEN LYING TO EACH OTHER

HEY! BABE! LET'S JUST CALL IT WHAT IT IS!
OIL AND WATER!
OIL AND WATER!
OIL AND WATER!
Now go away.
  (shoos away CHAD. CHAD walks away with his head down)

  AUGUST:

  (shocked)
That was putting it nicely? What has gotten into you?

  J.J.:

  (smiling)
Nothing yet, unlike you.
  AUGUST:

  (mortified)
I beg your pardon?

  J.J.:

  (smiling)
Tell me Gusto, how short is the list of the men you haven't
slept with? I know Rock's not on that list.

  AUGUST:

  (shouting)
You are such a bitch!
  *(storms away to the bar and sits down between LLEWELLYN and
  RICKY)*

  J.J.:

  (smirks)
Slut.

Beware

(LLEWELLYN looks up from his glass and notices AUGUST sitting next to him. He straightens up and clears his throat. He takes a sip of his beer before he speaks. He is wearing a blue checkered short-sleeved shirt and blue jeans with fire red cowboy boots)

LLEWELLYN:

What's up August.

AUGUST:

(looking towards the bar, not LLEWELLYN or RICKY)
Hey Lew.

LLEWELLYN:

Beware the beer they serve here. It's pretty close to water but it'll sneak up on you.
    (hiccups)

AUGUST:

Thanks for the heads up.

LLEWELLYN:

    (hiccups)
Buy you a drink?

AUGUST:

No thanks.
    (looks at RICKY. He nods)
Ricky's got it.

LLEWELLYN:

Well fine. Don' take my charity.

(takes a deep breath then sighs)
YOU SHOULD KNOW (BY NOW) REALLY
THAT THIS COULD END, REALLY
YOU SHOULD KNOW I COULD NEVER MAKE IT WORK
WAKE UP
LET'S PRETEND, REALLY
REALLY
BABE
(stands up and spills his drink. He reaches out to
AUGUST but she recoils into RICKY)
DO YOU LIKE THE WAY THE WATER TASTES
LIKE GUNFIRE
AND YOU KNEW BUT YOU COULD NEVER SAY
THEN COME FORTH 'CAUSE IT'S COMING ROUND
ROUND THE WATER
(he sits back down and points at AUGUST's drink, now
poured by PONY)
BEWARE THE WATER

YOU SHOULD KNOW
BABE
AT LEAST PRETEND YOU DID KNOW WHY
IT'S NOT LIKE YOU WATCH, SO GO ON TAKE A DRINK
REALLY
BABE

AUGUST:

Don't call me babe, Lew.

LLEWELLYN:

(ignores AUGUST)
DO YOU LIKE THE WAY THE WATER TASTES
LIKE GUNFIRE
YOU KNEW BUT IT WAS NEVER SAFE
TAKE ONE MORE 'CAUSE IT'S COMING ROUND
ROUND THE WATER

BEWARE THE WATER
BEWARE THE WATER
(reaches out to touch AUGUST on the shoulder)

RICKY:

(grabs *LLEWELLYN's arm and twists it*)
Back off, bro!

LLEWELLYN:

(*snaps his hand back and wipes it on his shirt*)
TEETH ARE DRY
FROM WIND BLOWS
IF YOU COME DRINKING
THERE YOU GO

BEWARE THE WATER
BEWARE THE WATER
(*turns away from AUGUST and orders another drink. PONY
shakes his head in refusal*)
BEWARE THE WATER
(*flips off PONY*)
DO YOU LIKE THE WAY THE WATER TASTES
DO YOU LIKE THE WAY THE WATER TASTES?

(*LLEWELLYN stands up and stumbles away from RICKY and
AUGUST towards STAGE RIGHT and the bathroom. He exits*)

Licking Cream

AUGUST:

(watches LLEWELLYN stumble away and turns towards RICKY)
He's drunker than usual. What's his deal?

RICKY:

(shrugs)
Whatever. Not my problem.

AUGUST:

That's not very nice!

RICKY:

(laughs)
I'm not his babysitter, Gus-…August.

AUGUST:

(angry)
What did you call me?!

RICKY:

(fumbles)
I said…
      (looks to PONY. He motions his hands in encouragement)
I……I wish you weren't so beautiful. In…my eyes.

AUGUST:

(startled)
Wh-wait, what?

      *[As RICKY begins to sing, it catches the attention of J.J.
      She watches the entire interaction with RICKY and AUGUST,
      growing increasingly agitated each time AUGUST touches*

*RICKY anywhere on his body. She says nothing but watches
intently]*

RICKY:

    (takes AUGUST's hand in his and takes a deep breath)
CORRUPT MY HOPE
IN JOYOUS HELL
BETWEEN THE LINES
LICK THE CREAM THAT SMELLS

    AUGUST:

What, you think I'm that easy?

    RICKY (AUGUST)

    (RICKY smiles)
I WISH YOU WEREN'T SO BEAUTIFUL IN MY EYES
    (AUGUST shrugs)
(CRAWLING DOWN YOUR SPINE TO MAKE YOU STAY)
    *(AUGUST stands up and walks behind RICKY to trace her
    fingers up and down his back)*
I WISH YOU WEREN'T SO BEAUTIFUL IN MY EYES
(COVERING YOUR EYES TO MAKE YOU PAY)
    *(RICKY stands and turns towards AUGUST. She balls her
    fist and pretends to punch him in the face)*

    AUGUST:

BEYOND THE HIGH
LIES BURNING EYES
CRASHED DOWN TO SOIL
FUCKED UP AND COILED

    RICKY (AUGUST):

I WISH YOU WEREN'T SO BEAUTIFUL IN MY EYES
(CRAWLING DOWN YOUR SPINE TO MAKE YOU STAY)
    (AUGUST runs her fingers down the front of his shirt)
I WISH YOU WEREN'T SO BEAUTIFUL IN MY EYES

(COVERING YOUR EYES TO MAKE YOU PAY)
        (she pretends to punch him in the stomach)

        RICKY:

        (pretends to recoil from her punch)
TOO BEAUTIFUL
TOO BEAUTIFUL
        (straightens his shimmering shirt)
YOU WANT TO FEEL IT
BUT YOU CAN'T REVEAL THAT
CONCEIVED THE MEANING
AND CARESS THE DEMON
        (touches himself)
ALL THOSE CALLOUS EYES
HOW THEY INFECT YOUR WORLD
SO YOU PRETEND TO REASON
BUT YOU'VE LOST YOUR SOUL
        (hovers his finger from her head to her torso)

        RICKY (AUGUST):

I WISH YOU WEREN'T SO BEAUTIFUL IN MY EYES
(CRAWLING DOWN YOUR SPINE TO MAKE YOU STAY)
        *(AUGUST grabs his shoulders and pulls him close for a
        hug)*
I WISH YOU WEREN'T SO BEAUTIFUL IN MY EYES
(COVERING YOUR EYES TO MAKE YOU PAY)
        *(AUGUST instead pulls him close to pretend-knee him in
        the crotch)*
YOU SHOULDN'T BE SO BEAUTIFUL IN MY EYES
(CRAWLING DOWN YOUR SPINE TO MAKE YOU STAY)
        *(AUGUST scowls and pushes him away; she starts walking away
from RICKY towards the audience)*
I WISH YOU WEREN'T SO BEAUTIFUL IN MY EYES
(COVERING YOUR EYES TO MAKE YOU PAY)
        *(RICKY recovers and grabs AUGUST by the arm before she
        could walk away)*
TOO BEAUTIFUL
TOO BEAUTIFUL
TOO BEAUTIFUL
TOO BEAUTIFUL
        (RICKY pulls her in close and kisses her on the mouth)

[J.J. stands at the end of RICKY's song and begins to walk towards ROCK and CHAD's table. She wants to dance]

Lose Yourself to Dance

    J.J.:

    (smiling)
Hey there, Rock. Want to dance?
    (leans on the table towards ROCK)

    ROCK:

    (looks up, surprised)
Dance? With you? I-I don't know if I should……
    (looks to CHAD)

    J.J.:

    (ignores CHAD's gaze)
I KNOW YOU DON'T GET A CHANCE TO TAKE A BREAK THIS OFTEN
I KNOW YOUR LIFE IS SPEEDING AND IT ISN'T STOPPING
    *(backs away from the table, swinging her hips and
    fingering at ROCK to join her on the dance floor)*
HERE TAKE MY SHIRT AND JUST GO AHEAD AND WIPE UP ALL THE
    (she plucks at the shoulders of her blouse)
SWEAT, SWEAT, SWEAT
    (she dips lower and lower with each 'sweat')

    [Her ballet talent begins to show as she twirls around to
    entice ROCK to come join her]

LOSE YOURSELF TO DANCE
LOSE YOURSELF TO DANCE
LOSE YOURSELF TO DANCE
LOSE YOURSELF TO DANCE
    *(she fingers at ROCK again. He reluctantly stands and
    follows J.J. onto the dance floor)*
LOSE YOURSELF TO DANCE
LOSE YOURSELF TO DANCE
LOSE YOURSELF TO DANCE
LOSE YOURSELF TO DANCE

ROCK:

(nods and smiles)
LOSE YOURSELF TO DANCE

J.J.:

(tugs on ROCK's shirt and pulls him close)
I KNOW YOU DON'T GET A CHANCE TO TAKE A BREAK THIS OFTEN
I KNOW YOUR LIFE IS SPEEDING AND IT ISN'T STOPPING
HERE TAKE MY SHIRT AND JUST GO AHEAD AND WIPE UP ALL THE
      (she begins to lift up her shirt as if to take it off
      Completely, revealing a red bra)
SWEAT, SWEAT, SWEAT
      (she drops her shirt and bends over into ROCK)

PONY (VIQI):

(motioning to other patrons towards the dance floor to
join ROCK and J.J.)
LOSE YOURSELF TO DANCE (COME ON)
LOSE YOURSELF TO DANCE (COME ON)
      [REPEATED]
LOSE YOURSELF TO DANCE (AT ALL)
LOSE YOURSELF TO DANCE (AT ALL)
      [REPEATED]

PONY:

(happily pouring drinks and dancing behind the bar
with VIQI)
EVERYBODY DANCING ON THE FLOOR
GETTING YOU READY FOR SOME MORE
EVERYBODY ON THE FLOOR
YEAH, COME ON
      [REPEATED]

[MARK MANN enters the club via STAGE LEFT, through the entrance. He stops just inside the entrance to watch J.J. and ROCK dance provocatively. He has in his hand, a clipboard adorned with gold pieces of paper. He is wearing the same uniform as before. No one notices him standing at the entrance]

(AUGUST takes notice of ROCK and J.J. dancing together. She reacts in surprise to see how aggressive J.J. is acting and dancing with ROCK and is equally angry. Seeing J.J. dancing with her crush sends a scowl across her face. RICKY attempts to catch her attention to no avail; AUGUST continues to watch, furious)

J.J.:

(holding ROCK close)
I KNOW YOU DON'T GET A CHANCE TO TAKE A BREAK THIS OFTEN
I KNOW YOUR LIFE IS SPEEDING AND IT ISN'T STOPPING
HERE TAKE MY SHIRT AND JUST GO AHEAD AND WIPE UP ALL THE
(puts ROCK's hands up her shirt, her hands up his shirt. It is revealed that his stomach is well toned with chiseled abs. J.J. is shocked and thrilled at the sight of his stomach and trails off)
Sweat, sweat, sweat……
(takes her finger from his chest and sticks it in her mouth, slowly sliding it out. She turns her head to make sure AUGUST and RICKY are paying attention before she then pulls ROCK close and kisses him passionately on the dance floor)

[MANN begins to walk slowly into club; no one notices him]

PONY (VIQI):

LOSE YOURSELF TO DANCE (COME ON)
LOSE YOURSELF TO DANCE (COME ON)
    [REPEATED]

(ROCK and J.J. break away. ROCK turns and notices MANN
standing behind him. He is mortified to see MANN standing
behind him. PONY continues to sing in the background but he
begins to trail off to allow MANN to sing)

LOSE YOURSELF TO DANCE (AT ALL)
LOSE YOURSELF TO DANCE (AT ALL)
     [REPEATED]

     PONY:

EVERYBODY DANCING ON THE FLOOR
GETTING YOU READY FOR SOME MORE
EVERYBODY ON THE FLOOR
YEAH, COME ON
LOSE YOURSELF TO DANCE......

(a hushed silence falls in the club. The music stops,
halted by VIQI. Everyone turns to see MANN standing before
ROCK and waits to see if MANN speaks. He will)

[**SET TRANSITION:** The lights descend upon the stage to allow
focus to be changed from the club dance floor to the
bathroom where LLEWELLYN resides, drunk and upset]

Hurt

[**SET TRANSITION:** *A well-lit and dressed bathroom. There are two stalls and a single urinal. A single sink with a tall mirror accompanies it; it is tall enough for a man to view his entire torso and face]*

(LLEWELLYN enters the MACINTOSH CLUB bathroom. He stumbles around the bathroom before he notices himself in the mirror that is atop a bathroom sink. The mirror is positioned facing STAGE RIGHT. The bathroom door enters/exits STAGE RIGHT)

LLEWELLYN:

(Sorrowful and drunk but not slurring his words)
I HURT MYSELF TODAY
TO SEE IF I STILL FEEL
I FOCUS ON THE PAIN
THE ONLY THING THAT'S REAL
THE NEEDLE TEARS A HOLE
THE OLD FAMILIAR STING
TRY TO KILL IT ALL AWAY
BUT I REMEMBER EVERYTHING

WHAT HAVE I BECOME
MY SWEETEST FRIEND
EVERYONE I KNOW GOES AWAY
IN THE END
AND YOU COULD HAVE IT ALL
MY EMPIRE OF DIRT
I WILL LET YOU DOWN
I WILL MAKE YOU HURT

(LLEWELLYN raises his fist as if to strike the mirror but lowers his arm at the last second. He begins to sing again)

I WEAR THIS CROWN OF THORNS
UPON MY LIAR'S CHAIR

(*LLEWELLYN wipes at his face, noticeably drunk*)

FULL OF BROKEN THOUGHTS
I CANNOT REPAIR
BENEATH THE STAINS OF TIME
THE FEELINGS DISAPPEAR
YOU ARE SOMEONE ELSE
I AM STILL RIGHT HERE

(*LLEWELLYN grips the sides of the sink*)

WHAT HAVE I BECOME
MY SWEETEST FRIEND
EVERYONE I KNOW GOES AWAY
IN THE END

(*LLEWELLYN raises his fist; he is left-handed*)

AND YOU COULD HAVE IT ALL
MY EMPIRE OF DIRT
I WILL LET YOU DOWN
I WILL MAKE YOU HURT

(*pause*)

(*LLEWELLYN slams his fist against the mirror. The mirror bends but does not break. LLEWELLYN cries out and shakes his hand*)

IF I COULD START AGAIN
A MILLION MILES AWAY

(*LLEWELLYN begins to laugh*)

I WOULD KEEP MYSELF
I WOULD FIND...A WAY

(*LLEWELLYN slips backwards from the mirror and turns towards a bathroom stall. He gives one last look towards the audience before he kneels and begins to throw up into the toilet*)

[**SET TRANSITION:** *The lighting fades out, casting the stage into darkness*]

[END SCENE]

The Pot

ROCK:

(stammers)
S-sir, I can explain!

MANN:

(says nothing, raises his hand to silence ROCK)

ROCK:

Whoa whoa, that's all I get? What do you think you're doing?
We're on our off time!
(points finger at MANN)

CHAD:

(in a warning tone)
Rock……

MANN:

*(moves his hand from ROCK to CHAD. CHAD sits back down. His
eyes never leave ROCK's)*

*[As MANN sings, he circles around ROCK like a vulture
circling its prey]*

WHO ARE YOU TO WAVE YOUR FINGER?
YA' MUST HAVE BEEN OUT YOUR HEAD.
EYE HOLE DEEP IN MUDDY WATERS.
YOU PRACTICALLY RAISED THE DEAD.
(points to AUGUST)
ROB THE GRAVE, TO SNOW THE CRADLE.
THEN BURN THE EVIDENCE DOWN.
(points to J.J.)
SOAPBOX, HOUSE OF CARDS, AND GLASS,
SO DON'T GO TOSSIN' YOUR STONES AROUND.

YOU MUST HAVE BEEN HIGH.
YOU MUST HAVE BEEN HIGH.
YOU MUST HAVE BEEN.
This is Colorado, after all.

        (points his finger into ROCK's chest)
FOOT IN MOUTH, AND HEAD UP ASSHOLE.
WHATCHA TALKIN' 'BOUT?
DIFFICULT TO DANCE 'ROUND THIS ONE
'TIL YOU PULL IT OUT, BOY!

YOU MUST HAVE BEEN, SO HIGH.
YOU MUST HAVE BEEN, SO HIGH.

STEAL, BORROW, REFER, SAVE YOUR SHADY INFERENCE.
KANGAROO DONE HUNG THE JUROR WITH THE INNOCENT.

NOW YOU'RE WEEPING SHADES OF COZENED INDIGO
GOT LEMON JUICE UP IN YOUR...EYE!
        (points to the yellow drinks on the table)
WHEN YOU PISSED ALL OVER MY BLACK KETTLE
YOU MUST HAVE BEEN HIGH, HIGH
YOU MUST HAVE BEEN HIGH, HIGH

WHO ARE YOU TO WAVE YOUR FINGER?
SO FULL OF IT.
EYEBALLS DEEP IN MUDDY WATERS
FUCKIN' HYPOCRITE.

        ROCK:

Wh-what?

        MANN:

What does it look like I'm doing, Eugene? I'm firing you.
        (hands ROCK a golden sheet and turns around to exit STAGE
        LEFT)

(ROCK (EUGENE) is stunned and speechless)

The Man Comes Around (Reprise)

[**SET TRANSITION:** *The set transitions back to the club; the dance floor, the bar, the entrance and the tables are all restored. All previous characters are restored to their previous stance]*

(RICKY stands up from the bar and walks over to the stunned ROCK. He places his arm around ROCK's shoulders and points to the entrance)

RICKY:

TILL ARMAGEDDON NO SHALAM, NO SHALOM.
THEN THE FATHER HEN WILL CALL HIS CHICKENS HOME,
THE WISE MAN WILL BOW DOWN BEFORE THE THRONE.
AND AT HIS FEET THEY'LL CAST THEIR GOLDEN CROWNS,
WHEN THE MAN COMES AROUND.
        (sweeps his arms across the club)
WHOEVER IS UNJUST LET HIM BE UNJUST STILL.
WHOEVER IS RIGHTEOUS LET HIM BE RIGHTEOUS STILL.
WHOEVER IS FILTHY LET HIM BE FILTHY STILL.
LISTEN TO THE WORDS LONG WRITTEN DOWN,
WHEN THE MAN COMES AROUND.
        (points back at the entrance)

[PONY re-enters the stage via STAGE RIGHT from the bathroom. He has blood on his hands and a panicked look on his face. He runs behind the bar to wash off his hands and whisper to VIQI about LLEWELLYN]

HEAR THE TRUMPETS, HEAR THE PIPERS.
ONE HUNDRED MILLION ANGELS SINGIN'.
MULTITUDES ARE MARCHIN' TO THE BIG KETTLEDRUM.
VOICES CALLIN', VOICES CRYIN'.
        (points to CHAD)
SOME ARE BORN AND SOME ARE DYIN'.
IT'S ALPHA AND OMEGA'S KINGDOM COME,

(points to PONY and VIQI)
AND THE WHIRLWIND IS IN THE THORN TREE.
THE VIRGINS ARE ALL TRIMMING THEIR WICKS,
        (points to J.J. and winks)
THE WHIRLWIND IS IN THE THORN TREES.
IT'S HARD FOR THEE TO KICK AGAINST THE PRICK,
        (he points to himself)
IN MEASURED HUNDREDWEIGHT AND PENNY POUND,
WHEN THE MAN COMES AROUND.
Tough luck, *Eugene!*
        *(slaps his hand against ROCK's back and walks away,
        laughing)*

        CHAD:

        (stands up and walks over to ROCK)
And I heard a voice in the midst of the four beasts. And I
looked, and behold a pale horse, and his name that sat on him
was Death, and hell followed with him.

        ROCK:

My……my life is over…

        CHAD:

Nah man, don't say that!

        ROCK:

I've…I've got nothing, Chad. Nothing! That job was my life…

        CHAD:

Forget about it, Rock. It's retail.
        (turns to PONY)
Pony, two shots of Jägermeister, stat!

        *(PONY nods in agreement and begins to pour two shots of
        Jägermeister)*

        (pause)

ROCK:

(sullen)
I guess you earned your man-card back.
(laughs weakly)

CHAD:

Come on, buddy. Grab a seat.

*(PONY delivers the shots himself along with one for
himself. His hands are clean)*

Gentleman, shot up!
*(all three men raise their glass, take the shot, then slam
the glasses on the table)*

ROCK:

(winces)
So…what now?

(pause)

PONY:

Now…
(looks at VIQI. She nods)
We close!

*(all in the bar protests. PONY waves his hands to calm down
the clamoring crowd)*
I know, I know. But we've come to the end.
(he sweeps his arm to corral the patrons)
Come on, come on!

CHAD:

Where are we supposed to go?

PONY:

(shrugs)
Just follow the lights home.
(shouts)
Line up!

*[Everyone in the bar lines up in front of the audience.
Everyone except LLEWELLYN. A bright spotlight illuminates
the entrance to the bar, signifying its exit]*

Fix You

LLEWELLYN:

(off stage)
WHEN YOU TRY YOUR BEST, BUT YOU DON'T SUCCEED

J.J.:

(embracing ROCK)
WHEN YOU GET WHAT YOU WANT, BUT NOT WHAT YOU NEED

CHAD:

WHEN YOU FEEL SO TIRED, BUT YOU CAN'T SLEEP

ROCK:

STUCK IN REVERSE

LLEWELLYN:

(off stage)
AND THE TEARS COME STREAMING DOWN YOUR FACE

J.J.:

(pushes away ROCK)
WHEN YOU LOSE SOMETHING YOU CAN'T REPLACE

AUGUST:

*(a physical distance appears between RICKY and AUGUST.
AUGUST looks to the distance; RICKY averts his eyes from
AUGUST)*
WHEN YOU LOVE SOMEONE, BUT IT GOES TO WASTE

ROCK:

COULD IT BE WORSE?

PONY:

   (pointing to the entrance)
LIGHTS WILL GUIDE YOU HOME

   VIQI:

AND IGNITE YOUR BONES

   PONY:

   (looking towards the restroom, STAGE RIGHT)
AND I WILL TRY TO FIX YOU

   VIQI:

AND HIGH UP ABOVE OR DOWN BELOW

   CHAD:

   (looking to J.J., a pained look on his face)
WHEN YOU'RE TOO IN LOVE TO LET IT GO
BUT IF YOU NEVER TRY YOU'LL NEVER KNOW

   ROCK:

JUST WHAT YOU'RE WORTH

   VIQI:

LIGHTS WILL GUIDE YOU HOME
AND IGNITE YOUR BONES

   AUGUST:

AND I WILL TRY TO FIX YOU

   *(LLEWELLYN returns on stage; he is wiping at his face. He
   stands at the end of the line)*

CHORUS:

TEARS STREAM DOWN YOUR FACE
WHEN YOU LOSE SOMETHING YOU CANNOT REPLACE
TEARS STREAM DOWN YOUR FACE
AND I...

TEARS STREAM DOWN YOUR FACE
I PROMISE YOU I WILL LEARN FROM MY MISTAKES
TEARS STREAM DOWN YOUR FACE
AND I...

PONY:

LIGHTS WILL GUIDE YOU HOME
AND IGNITE YOUR BONES

AUGUST:

AND I WILL TRY TO FIX YOU

[Final curtain]

ABOUT THE AUTHOR

James Pavlick is a published author based in Boulder, Colorado. When he's not writing, he's taking in the scenery with hiking and biking. He is active in the community and would someday like to travel far and away for his next adventure.

www.ingramcontent.com/pod-product-compliance
Lightning Source LLC
Chambersburg PA
CBHW080835160726

47999CB00009B/2892